GHOST HUNT

GHOST HUNT

Chilling Tales of the Unknown

BY JASON HAWES AND GRANT WILSON
WITH CAMERON DOKEY

SCHOLASTIC INC.
New York Toronto London Auckland
Sydney Mexico City New Delhi Hong Kong

The events in this book are based on real investigations by the authors, Jason Hawes and Grant Wilson. However, the authors have fictionalized the stories, and any similarity to actual events or people, living or dead, is coincidental and not intended by the authors.

ISBN 978-0-545-41990-1

12 11 10 9 8 7 6 5 4   14 15 16/0

Printed in the U.S.A.   40

First Scholastic printing, October 2011

I dedicate this book to my ever-loving wife and true friend, Reanna, and my loving boys, Connor, Noah, and Jonah. You have been with me through the thickest and the thinnest and always support me, comfort me, teach me, and laugh with me. I could never find truer friends nor closer family. I look forward to an eternity spent in great company.

—GRANT WILSON

This book is dedicated to my wife, Kristen. Thank you for standing beside me and allowing me to follow my dreams, and helping me with making all things possible. To my children, Samantha, Haily, Satori, Austin, and Logan. You have showed me what it is to be young at heart again. You have also all shown me how to be a father and a friend. I love you!

—JASON HAWES

TABLE OF CONTENTS

INTRODUCTION

Here's an easy question: Do you like ghost stories?

Of course you do. Everyone likes a good ghost story. Everyone gets chills from stories about a mournful voice that whispers one name over and over again...

A face that appears from nowhere and then disappears in an instant...

An invisible hand that reaches out of the darkness and grabs you...

We've all heard stories like these. Maybe your older brother told you a ghost story to scare you when you were much younger. Maybe *you* told a ghost story to scare *him*! Or maybe you sat around a flickering campfire and listened with all your friends to a creepy story and were scared together.

People have always told ghost stories, but the stories in this book are different. These stories are our job.

Our job is to go into places that might be haunted and look for ghosts or other evidence of paranormal activity. *Paranormal* means "beyond normal."

For example, let's say you hear a knocking sound in your room at night. If the noise comes from a broken shutter that hits the side of the house when the wind blows—that's normal. But what if there is no normal reason, no banging shutter? You try but you can't find any reason for that sound. Then it's possible that the reason is paranormal. Maybe the sound was made by a ghost.

Our job is to look for evidence. We have been investigating cases and looking at evidence for a long time. We started an organization called The Atlantic Paranormal Society (TAPS), and now we do some of our investigations on a TV show called *Ghost Hunters*.

Along the way, we've come across some amazing ghost stories. We have picked out some of the most interesting ones to share with you in this book.

Some of these stories are mysteries that we had to solve. *Why don't the ghosts that Bill sees have legs?* The answer will amaze you.

Other stories are really sad. *Why does a child's voice call out in the darkness of an old Army fort?*

And some of the stories are truly scary. Just wait until you read "Ghost on the Water." It is guaranteed to give you a chill.

The stories in this book are all different from one another—but they have one thing in common: they are all based on what really happened when we did our investigations. An invisible hand really did try to push Grant off a ladder, and we really did see a face in a dark dungeon.

Go to www.GhostHuntBooks.com and you will be able to hear and see some of the amazing evidence from the cases for yourself!

Then check out the *Ghost Hunt* Guide in the back of this book. It will show you how to do your own investigation. Who knows? Maybe the next ghost story you tell will be your *own*.

Good luck!

JASON HAWES and GRANT WILSON

PENNIES FROM A GHOST

There's nothing to be afraid of, Scott Briscoe thought.

For the last five minutes, maybe more, Scott had been standing in the hall just outside his own bedroom. His hands and feet felt like heavy bricks. He couldn't move. His stomach was full of butterflies. Actually, whatever was causing his stomach to churn felt a whole lot bigger than butterflies. He couldn't bring himself to turn the doorknob and go back into his room.

Okay. Stop acting like a stupid wimp, Scott told himself. Still, stupid was better than another word he could think of that started with the letter *s*.

S for scared.

The truth is, he was terrified. Weird things were happening

3

all over Scott's house. But the stuff that happened in the room he shared with his older brother, Jerry—that was the weirdest stuff of all.

Scott had gotten up to go to the bathroom. And now here he was in the hall, afraid to go back into his own bedroom.

I have to go in there, he told himself. *I can't leave Jerry all alone.*

Scott took a deep breath. *I'm going in on three,* he thought.

One. Scott's right arm came up. His hand reached out toward the door.

Two. He wrapped his fingers around the doorknob. Slowly, feeling as if it took super-human strength, he turned the doorknob to the right.

Three! With a burst of energy, Scott pushed open the door. Quickly, before he could chicken out, he stepped into the room and closed the door behind him.

Click.

It's so dark! Scott thought. Too dark. Why wasn't the nightlight on? It was on five minutes ago when he got up. Who—or what—had turned it off?

"*Scott.*"

The whisper snaked through the room like a current of cold air. Scott shivered. He took a step back. Just one step. That's as far as he could go. He felt the doorknob digging into his back.

"*Scott.*"

"I'm not afraid of you," Scott said in a loud voice.

"Are you nuts, or what?" Jerry whispered. "It's only me. And keep your voice down."

"How come?" Scott whispered this time too. "And what happened to the light?"

"I turned it off."

"Why?"

"I want to try and catch *it*," Jerry said. "I didn't want the light to scare it off."

"*You want to try and catch it?*" Scott echoed. "And *you're* calling *me* nuts?"

"We have to catch it," Jerry answered. "It's the only way to make the weird stuff stop."

"But *how* are we going to catch it?" Scott asked. "We don't even know what *it* is. We only know what it leaves behind: pennies."

Pennies that appeared out of nowhere on their bedroom floor.

Pennies that were always arranged in a deliberate design.

Pennies that told Scott and his brother they were not alone.

"I don't know how we're going to catch it," Jerry confessed. "I was waiting for you to come back so we could figure it out together."

Slowly, arms out in front of him, barely picking up his feet as he walked, Scott felt his way across the dark room.

Bump. His right knee collided with the side of his bed. Scott turned around and sat down, hard. His heart was pounding, the way it did when he ran the hundred-yard dash.

"Maybe we should sleep in the living room."

"No way," Jerry said. "This is our room. It's up to us."

Jerry had a point. And now that his eyes were used to the dark, Scott felt a little better. A glow came in from the big streetlight at the end of the intersection. Scott twisted around. He could just make out Jerry, huddled in the bed next to his.

"Maybe we should think like Spock," he suggested. Scott was a huge *Star Trek* fan, but Jerry was all about *Star Wars*. "We should try and be logical. Let's name all the places where the pennies showed up. That way, maybe we can figure out where *it* will go next. Then we can set a trap or something."

"Okay," Jerry said. "That's good. I like it. Last time they were at the end of my bed."

"In front of the dresser before that," Scott said, continuing the list.

"And before that, outside the closet," Jerry went on. "But the first time…"

The first time was the creepiest of all, Scott thought.

The pennies were by his bed that time, on the side where he always got in and out. He put his bare feet right on them. The room was very warm, but the coins were as cold as ice.

"I don't think the list is helping," Jerry said.

Scott had to agree. The pennies showed up all over the place. It was impossible to figure out exactly where they would turn up next. But one thing they knew for sure: the pennies only showed up in *their* room.

"So now what?" he asked.

"Well—" Jerry began. He broke off. His head swiveled toward the window.

"What's that? Did you hear that?" he asked in a tense voice.

Scott nodded. He wanted to say something, but he couldn't talk past the giant lump of fear in his throat.

The sound grew louder, *louder*, LOUDER. A deep throaty rumble. *Like thunder*, Scott thought. But it wasn't thunder.

Without warning, a burst of light appeared on the wall across from the boys' beds. Scott heard Jerry make a strangled sound. The light flickered. It seemed to hover in the same place.

Then it began to slide along the wall.

It's looking for something! Scott thought. *It's looking for Jerry and me.*

The light was almost to the bed now. Another minute and it would…

"A truck," Jerry choked out. "That's all it is. It's a truck."

Scott bolted out of bed and dashed to the window. He was just in time to see an old pickup rumble past the house. It was heading away from town.

Scott turned away from the window, back toward his

bed—and felt a shiver of pure ice shoot straight down his spine. He tried to speak, but the only word he could get out was: *"Jerry!"*

"No way," Jerry said at once.

Scott knew he didn't have to say any more. He heard the rustle of covers as Jerry got out of bed. Jerry walked over to the window and stood next to Scott.

On the floor in front of the window, barely visible in the glow of the streetlight, were seven coins. Seven pennies. Six arranged in a circle with the seventh in the middle.

"It's the same shape as before," Jerry said. "Like a daisy."

"But this time is different," Scott said slowly, thinking hard about what he was about to say. "They weren't there when we went to bed. We checked the whole room. Right?"

"Right," Jerry said.

"So that means that whatever put those pennies here could have done it just a little while ago."

"Yeah," Jerry agreed.

"And it also means that whatever put those pennies here could be here *right now!*"

Brrring. Brrriing.

Lyssa Frye jumped. Her pen flew from her fingers and sailed

across the room. It landed with a *smack* on Grant Wilson's desk. Papers flew off onto the floor.

Brrriing. Brriiiiinng.

Lyssa looked around the TAPS office. She had several weeks of training, but today was different. Today was her first day as an official member of The Atlantic Paranormal Society.

It's like the first day at a new school, she thought. *That's the nervous feeling I have.*

Like the first day at a new school. Only this was a job. Here she was, with her own desk.

People called TAPS when they were in trouble. They called when they heard or saw frightening things in their houses. Were they living with ghosts? Were they living in a *haunted house*?

Sometimes people didn't know what to think. They were afraid they were going crazy.

Brriiinngg. Brrriinnnggg.

Lyssa cleared her throat and forced herself to pick up the phone. "The Atlantic Paranormal Society. How can I help you?" she said.

The woman on the other end of the phone started talking loud and fast. She was so loud that Lyssa pulled the phone away from her ear.

"Okay, Mrs. Briscoe," Lyssa said. "Yes, I understand why you're upset."

Lyssa tucked the phone against her shoulder and dug out

another pen. Then she flipped to a clean page on her yellow notepad.

"Let me just get some basic info from you, all right? Please give me your address and phone number. And tell me the names of the other people who live in your house."

Still listening, Lyssa began to write.

Lyssa learned this during her training: first ask the really easy questions. Easy questions help people calm down. *Then* you can ask them about the stuff that freaked them out.

It worked. The woman on the phone lowered her voice and stopped talking so fast.

"Thank you," Lyssa said as she finished jotting down the address. "You say that's out in the country? In southern Massachusetts? Good. That's close to us. We're in Rhode Island, you know.

"All right, now that I have all that," Lyssa continued, "let's talk about the reason for your call. Your sons think there is a ghost in your house?" She paused. "Yes. I see why they are so frightened."

A blast of chilly air made Lyssa look up. She turned toward the open door in time to see Jason Hawes and Grant Wilson walk in.

Grant gave her a thumbs-up. Jason flashed her a smile. They walked quietly across the room to their desks. Lyssa mouthed a quick "I'm sorry" as Grant knelt to pick up the papers on the floor.

Jason and Grant were the two guys who started TAPS. They wanted to help people who thought they were having a paranormal experience.

Lyssa remembered how Jason explained it to her. "*Paranormal* means *beyond* the normal," he said. "Strange visions, weird sounds, objects appearing and disappearing—weird stuff that can upset and frighten people."

"So we go investigate," Jason told her. "Sometimes we find paranormal things going on. Sometimes we even find evidence of a ghost. But that's not our first job. Our first job is to try to help people feel less scared and upset."

Lyssa had gasped in surprise the first time she saw the TAPS office. "It's an old house," she said. "A very tiny old house."

A funny thought had flashed into her mind then: *Maybe it's haunted by very tiny old ghosts!*

But then Lyssa looked around. The living room of the house had been turned into the main work area. It didn't look like a spooky place at all.

The walls were painted a creamy white and decorated with maps from all over the country. Lyssa liked the big brick fireplace on one wall.

Jason's and Grant's desks stood on either side of the fireplace, facing each other. Lyssa guessed this made it easier for them to talk about the cases.

Lyssa's new desk stood on the other side of the room. She and Jennifer Shorewood, the technical manager, would work side by side.

The other two members of the TAPS team, Mike and Mark Hammond, shared a big worktable along the back wall. The Hammonds were identical twins, both tall and serious-looking, with dark eyes and straight brown hair. Mike studied evidence the team collected. Mark researched the places they investigated.

Lyssa was afraid to admit that she couldn't tell them apart, even after several weeks. Was Mark the one with longer hair? Was Mike the one who kept sneaking looks at Jen?

"All right, Mrs. Briscoe," Lyssa said into the phone. "I think I have everything I need for now. I'll tell your story to the rest of the team, and we'll get back to you as soon as we can."

Lyssa hung up the phone.

"Your first phone call," Jason said. "Someone in trouble. How did that make you feel?"

"No problem," Lyssa said. *No way* would she admit she was almost too nervous to answer the phone!

Grant leaned forward. His dark eyes stared into Lyssa's.

"Why don't you tell us what that was all about?"

"Wow," Mark Hammond said the next afternoon. He stared out the front window of the SUV. For once, his hair didn't flop down into his eyes. That's because both he and Mike were wearing Red Sox baseball caps.

"This place really is in the middle of nowhere."

"I wouldn't go that far," Mike piped up from the backseat.

"We *did* go that far," Mark joked.

"Ha, ha. Very funny," Mike said.

Lyssa didn't think that was all that funny, but she laughed anyway. The way the twins talked to each other cracked her up. They finished each other's sentences and laughed at the same things. They really were identical in every way.

"Didn't you guys grow up in the country?" Lyssa asked, keeping her eyes on the road. She was driving one of the team's SUVs. Another first.

Lyssa steered the SUV around a bend in the road. Up ahead, she could see the back of the equipment van that Jen was driving. Grant and Jason were in the lead in their own SUV.

"We did grow up in the country," Mark said now. "In southern Vermont. And before you ask, the stories are all true."

Lyssa snuck a glance in his direction. "Really? You guys actually grew up in a haunted house?"

"Yep," Mike piped up. "You could say the two of us have been Ghost Hunters since we were kids."

At that moment, Lyssa heard the crackle of static.

"SUV One to all team members," a voice said. "This is Jason. Do you copy?"

Mike picked up the walkie-talkie and pushed the button on the side. "Mike here. Go ahead. Over."

Lyssa glanced in the rearview mirror. Mike was grinning from ear to ear. He loved using the walkie-talkie.

"Just checking in," Jason said. "Everybody clear on the Briscoe details?"

In the front seat, both Mark and Lyssa nodded. This was Ghost Hunters SOP, standard operating procedure. Jason or Grant always did one last check-in right before arriving at a site.

"I think we're good, Jay," Mike said into the walkie-talkie. "The reports include a lot of the usual: moving shadows, voices. Also, the parents report a general creepy feeling in the basement."

"Basements give *me* the creeps in general," Lyssa muttered.

"Don't forget the pennies," Mark said. "They show up in the boys' room practically every night."

"Right," Mike said. "The pennies. That's got me pretty curious, I have to admit."

"I'm sure we all agree on that," Jason's voice said. "We've got a lot to focus on for this one, guys."

"Right," Mike said. "Can't wait to get at it!"

"Copy that," Jason said. "ETA is about two minutes. See you there. SUV one over and out."

Mike switched off the walkie-talkie and stowed it in his backpack. Then he took off his baseball cap and stowed that too. A lock of hair flopped down into his eyes and he pushed it back. Lyssa caught the movement in the rearview mirror.

"Hey, wait a minute!" she cried. "You're not Mike, you're Mark!"

The real Mike began to laugh. He took off his cap too. The twins had pulled a switch. Lyssa had been completely fooled.

"Man," Mark said. "I love it when we get somebody new."

The Briscoe house was two stories tall, white with green shutters. It had a wide front porch and a driveway shaped like a half circle in front. The house was set back a short distance from the road. There were two trees in the front yard. Their branches swayed in the late-afternoon breeze.

Lyssa stared up at the house. She could feel her heart start to pound. This was it. The very first place she'd investigate as an official TAPS team member.

I can do this. I really want *to do this,* she thought.

She turned off the engine. All three of them got out of the SUV. The twins headed over to the equipment van right away.

Lyssa paused. In one of the upstairs windows, she saw a sudden flash of light.

"What was that?" she said, trying to sound calm. "Did anybody else see that?"

"See what?"

Jen Shorewood came to Lyssa's side.

"I thought I saw a flash of light in one of the upstairs windows," Lyssa said. She squinted up at the house. "It's gone now."

"We can check it out when we get inside," Jen suggested.

"Okay." Lyssa nodded. "Let me give you a hand. Unless the twins grabbed all the stuff."

Jen smiled. "How was the ride? I love working with them. They're so funny."

"Funny, right," Lyssa said as they walked to the equipment van. "They pulled a switch. I called Mark *Mike* and Mike *Mark* the whole ride out. They had baseball caps on so I couldn't see their hair. That's the only way I can tell them apart."

"You got off easy," Jen said. "They must like you. The last newbie we had was a guy. They kept the switch going for a week."

"Good to know!" Lyssa picked up a laptop case in one hand. Jen watched her as she slung a roll of cable over her shoulder.

"You look like you've been doing this forever," Jen said. She picked up two more cases and they walked toward the house. "Nervous?" Jen asked.

"A little," Lyssa admitted. "I want to do a good job."

"Jason and Grant think you have what it takes," Jen said. "You wouldn't have made the team otherwise. Still…" She paused. "I remember my first case. I was so scared I couldn't keep my hands from shaking. Totally embarrassing."

Lyssa smiled. All of a sudden, she felt much better.

A short flight of steps led up to the Briscoes' front porch. Grant knocked on the door. It flew open almost before he was finished knocking. Two boys with bright red hair and curious green eyes stood just inside. They were dressed in faded jeans. The older boy wore a green T-shirt, and the younger boy wore a blue one.

"Are you here to catch the ghost?" the taller of the two boys asked.

That's Jerry, Lyssa thought.

"We're here to investigate," Jason answered. "To take a look around and see if we can figure out what's going on."

"But you're called Ghost Hunters," Jerry protested.

"And besides, we already *know* what's going on," the younger boy spoke up.

And that's Scott, Lyssa thought.

"It *has* to be a ghost," Scott went on. "Jerry and I figured it out. We used logic and everything, just like Mr. Spock."

"Easy, there, Scotty," a tall man said, appearing behind the boys. He laid a firm but gentle hand on Scott's shoulder. "No need to go to maximum warp right off. These people came a long way. How about we ask them to come inside?"

17

"Oh, yeah," Scott said. "Sorry."

"Duh," Jerry muttered.

Scott's face turned a dull red. "Duh yourself."

"I'm Henry Briscoe," the tall man said. With Jason and Grant in the lead, the TAPS team entered the house. "You've already met the boys. My wife, Janet, will be out in a minute."

Henry Briscoe led them to the dining room. "We'll take you on a tour of the house. But I'm thinking you might like to put your equipment here." He pointed to the dining room table.

"Great," Grant said.

"Are you going to use all that stuff?" Jerry pointed to the cases and cables.

"Yep," Jen said, nodding.

"But what is it?" Scott asked.

"Well," Jason answered, "we have cameras and voice recorders. They're both digital, so we download any evidence they collect to one of Jen's computers. That way, we can go over it later, back at the office. This is Jen. She's our technical manager."

"Hi." Jen gave the boys a smile. She opened a case and took out something that looked sort of like a TV remote.

"We use these too. They're EMF detectors. EMF stands for electromagnetic field."

Jen shot an encouraging glance in Lyssa's direction.

"Electromagnetic energy is kind of like an invisible force

field," Lyssa explained. "Lots of things give it off. Things that have nothing to do with ghosts. Like, say, your refrigerator."

"But sometimes it *might* be a ghost," Scott insisted.

"Yes," Lyssa said. "Sometimes. That's why we like to carry these. If we get a big reading and there's no electrical stuff in sight, we know there might be more to investigate."

"Can we help you set up?" Jerry asked.

"Thanks for the offer, guys," Jason said. "But that's something we need to handle ourselves. Tell you what, though. You can take Lyssa here"—he put a hand on her arm to show who he meant—"upstairs to your room and tell her what's been going on. That will help us decide where to place our cameras."

"Outstanding," Scott said. "Come on. Let's go."

Lyssa followed the boys into their room. She saw two twin beds, two dressers, two desks. Colorful movie posters covered the walls. She sat on one of the beds—and saw a quick flash of light.

"What's that?" She jumped up.

Jerry rolled his eyes. "Crystals," he said in a disgusted tone. "Mom made us put them up."

"They're always doing that flashing thing," Scott volunteered. "And sometimes they make rainbows on the walls."

Lyssa pulled a small notebook out of her back pocket. "I should write that down." She made a quick note. She turned on her digital recorder and said, "Okay, guys. Why don't you show me where you've seen the pennies."

"We thought you'd want to know that," Scott said, his tone proud. "So we marked them."

He pointed to the rug.

Lyssa grinned. "I was wondering about all that masking tape stuck to the rug. So, X marks the spot."

"Spots," Jerry corrected her.

"Right. This is really nice work, guys. I'll make sure Grant and Jason know you did this."

"Cool," said Scott.

Lyssa walked around the room, studying each location. There were five in all.

"Have the pennies ever shown up in the same place twice?" she asked.

Jerry shook his head. "Nope."

"What did you do with the pennies?" she asked.

"We saved them," Scott said. He walked to one of the twin beds. Then, to Lyssa's surprise, he got down on his hands and knees. He pulled a jam jar out from underneath the bed. Then he scrambled up and brought it over to her.

"Here."

Lyssa reached out and took the jam jar. All her senses seemed to tingle. *I'm holding my first real piece of evidence,* she thought.

Did a ghost really leave these pennies? She was about to find out.

It was 11:00 PM, a time when most people are asleep—but not TAPS people. For TAPS, nighttime is ghost hunt time.

Jason, Grant, Jen, the twins, and Lyssa stood in the dimly lit dining room, where they had set up the TAPS Central Command Center. That's the place where the team can meet and get instructions from Jason and Grant. Lyssa saw several computer monitors on the table. They allowed the people in the Command Center to see where all the team members were during the investigation.

"Okay, everybody," Jason said. "In just a few minutes we're going to go dark. If you have any last-minute questions, now's the time to speak up."

This is it, Lyssa thought. *The moment I've been waiting for.*

The Briscoe family was upstairs. The boys were sleeping in their parents' room for the night.

"Grant and Mark will stay on the main floor. Jen and Mike, take the upstairs," Jason continued. "Lyssa and I will check out the basement."

Lyssa's heart sank. She suddenly felt sick to her stomach. She hated basements. They were small and dark—one of her least favorite combinations. She felt a tiny bead of sweat roll down the center of her back.

Keep it together, Lyssa, she told herself.

"Let's all make a first sweep, then come back here," Jason said. "Everybody set?"

Along with the rest of the team, Lyssa nodded. There was no way she was going to confess that small dark places made her want to puke.

"All right, then," Grant said. "We're going dark in five, four, three, two…*one.*"

"Let's start by taking some EMF readings," Jason said. He and Lyssa crept down the basement stairs. Lyssa's heart pounded. She felt as if she were running up the stairs instead of walking down.

Just keep going. You can do this, she told herself. Still, she was seriously glad Jason was first in line.

"Okay," Jason said in a low voice. "I'm at the bottom. Do you have the camera ready?"

"Ready," Lyssa said. If the EMF detector picked up anything, it was Lyssa's job to take a picture of the hot spot. She was ready. She just wished her hands would stop shaking.

Lyssa reached the bottom of the stairs. Her chest felt tight. Her head was pounding like a hammer. Her skin felt itchy, like there were bugs crawling on it. She resisted the temptation to scratch her arms. Instead, she switched on her flashlight. The thin beam of light made her feel a little better.

"That's interesting," Jason said suddenly.

"What?"

"I'm getting a pretty high reading," Jason said.

Lyssa peered around Jason's arm. The first four LED lights on his EMF detector glowed bright red.

"Do you know where it's coming from?"

"Not yet," Jason answered. "Let's do a sweep. Watch your step. The floor looks kind of rough."

They began to walk around the basement. Lyssa aimed her flashlight beam in front of Jason so he could see where he was going. As he walked, Jason slowly moved the EMF detector up and down and side to side.

Lyssa could hear someone breathing loudly, in and out. In and out. Then she realized she was doing it herself. The air in the basement was cold, and it had a weird, sour, damp smell.

"How are you doing?" Jason asked.

"Fine," Lyssa said at once. She didn't want to tell Jason she was freaking out.

"I'm going to try making contact," Jason said. He stopped walking.

"Okay," Lyssa said, and nodded. *Here goes,* she thought.

"Hello," Jason said, raising his voice a little. "My name is Jason Hawes, and this is Lyssa Frye. The Briscoe family asked us to come and spend some time in their house. Some pretty unusual things are going on. We're here to see if we can understand why.

"If there's anybody in the basement with us, will you please give us a sign?"

Silence. All of a sudden, Lyssa realized she was holding her breath. The basement walls felt like they were pressing in on her. *It's like being in a tomb,* she thought.

"We mean you no harm. We just want to know if you're here," Jason went on. He resumed his walk around the basement, holding the EMF meter out in front of him. "If there's someone here, can you give us a sign?"

Nothing, Lyssa thought. Just the beam of her flashlight and the red glow from Jason's EMF detector. As she stared at it, a shiver crept down Lyssa's spine. The meter showed five lights now. One more than before.

"Why don't you try?" Jason suggested in a low voice.

Lyssa's throat was so dry, she wasn't sure she could make any sound come out.

"Hello," she croaked. She cleared her throat, then tried again. "Like Jason said, my name is Lyssa, and, um…"

This is harder than it looks! Lyssa realized suddenly. She was talking to the dark. She was asking a ghost to show itself. Most people would be running the other way.

But I'm not most people. I'm a TAPS investigator. Or at least she was trying to be one.

24

"I'm going to set my flashlight down on the floor," she went on. "If you're with us, will you make the flashlight roll? It's not very heavy. I'm sure you can do it if you try."

She crouched and placed the flashlight on the cold cement floor.

"Whoa," Jason suddenly said.

Lyssa stood up fast. "What?"

Jason held the EMF detector out so Lyssa could see it. Ten LED lights were showing now! This was the biggest EMF reading Lyssa had ever seen. Suddenly she began to shiver uncontrollably. She rubbed her hands up and down her arms.

"But the flashlight hasn't moved," she whispered.

"No," Jason agreed. "But something's definitely going on. We need to find the hot spot."

"Okay," Lyssa said. "I'll get the flashlight."

Lyssa took a step toward the flashlight, then stumbled on the basement's uneven floor. With a cry, she pitched forward. Her toe caught the flashlight, sending it spinning away. Over and over it turned, the beam of light making crazy circles on the ceiling and walls.

"Oh, no!" Lyssa cried.

The flashlight stopped. The beam winked out. The basement was plunged into total darkness.

"That's okay. Everything's okay," Jason said quickly. "I think I can use the light from the EMF detector to find the flashlight. Stay where you are."

Hurry! Please hurry! Lyssa thought. Her heart pounded. She hated this creepy basement.

She heard Jason move away. The red LED lights danced before her eyes like spots.

"Got it," Jason grunted. The red lights dipped as Jason knelt. A moment later, the flashlight beam came back on.

"Oh, thank goodness!" Lyssa cried out. She was relieved— but embarrassed. Now Jason knew how nervous she was.

"You're not kidding," Jason agreed. He handed her the flashlight. Lyssa gripped it tightly. "I don't really like small, dark spaces," Jason went on. "Never have."

Lyssa let out a nervous giggle. "I don't like them, either," she said. "I was having kind of a hard time being brave about it."

"So we're even, then," Jason said. "Don't be afraid to admit you're scared, Lyssa. We all are sometimes. Now let's see if we can find that hot spot."

Lyssa and Jason made their way to the far corner of the basement.

"There, you see that?" Jason asked. "That's the breaker box. Now check out the EMF readings."

"Still off the charts."

"Right. There's a problem with this box. It's leaking electricity. You know, a high EMF like this can sometimes affect people.

The high electronic field can make some people feel sick. Or it can make people feel nervous and strange. Maybe that's what the Briscoes were feeling."

"I know it made *me* feel strange," Lyssa admitted.

"Me too," Jason said. "I'm going to recommend they get an electrician in here. We'll do a follow-up, but I think we can rule out the paranormal in the basement for now."

He turned away from the breaker box. "Let's head back upstairs. I wonder how Jen and Mike are doing in the boys' room."

Me too, Lyssa thought.

"Do you see any pennies?" Mike asked.

He stood in the doorway of Scott and Jerry's room, shining his flashlight around at the walls.

"Not yet," Jen said. She took a few steps inside the room. "But you know, Mike, I'm thinking they're going to be on the *floor*."

"Yeah, okay, I know that," Mike said. He aimed the flashlight beam at the light blue carpet. "Just trying to get a sense of the space, that's all."

"This is Jen and Mike," Jen said so the video camera would pick it up. "The time is 11:10 PM. We're beginning our investigation of the boys' room."

Mike swept the flashlight beam across the boys' beds, then over toward the window. The last place Jerry and Scott found the pennies was right in front of it. As he moved the beam across the window, the room suddenly seemed to explode with light. Jen threw a hand up to cover her eyes.

"Whoa," Mike exclaimed. "Did you see that? What *was* that?"

"I don't know. But we should definitely check it out. Go slowly, though."

Carefully, walking on tiptoe, as if they were cats stalking mice, Jen and Mike crossed the room. They were almost at the window.

"Okay," Mike said in a low voice. "Shine your flashlight on the window again."

Jen ran the flashlight beam across the window. There was a second explosion of light. All of a sudden, Mike laughed.

"Oh, I see now. It's those crystals Lyssa mentioned. I should have remembered about those. They're reflecting the light from our flashlights. That explains that."

"Uh-huh." Jen nodded. "Weird flashes of light, check. But those crystals don't explain the other weird things."

They turned away from the window and looked around the room. A low howl sent a shiver down Jen's spine. "Look. The wall," she said, pointing to the space above Scott's bed.

Jen saw strange dark shapes. They looked like long arms with big claws. Shadows. The Briscoes said they saw shadows. *Okay, but shadows of what?* The shadows flickered in and out in rhythm with the eerie howls.

"What is that sound?" Mike asked.

Jen turned and gazed out the window. "I think it's just the wind." She watched the tree branches in the yard bend under the wind's force. "The light from the streetlight is causing the shadows. But it only happens when the wind is strong enough to blow the branches in front of the light. The combination of the howl and those shadows could scare anybody. But there's no ghost here."

"Jen, you're wrong," Mike said.

"No, Mike. It's the wind." She turned around—and gasped.

Mike stood between the two beds, staring down at the floor. He was staring at a flower made of seven pennies.

"This afternoon we're going to review the evidence on the Briscoe case," Grant said.

It was about a week later. The entire TAPS team sat around a big table in the back room of the TAPS office. Jen had her laptop up and running, ready to play back the evidence recorded at the Briscoe home.

The team had spent three nights at the house. Every night, pennies appeared in Scott and Jerry's bedroom.

"We were able to debunk a lot of what the family was experiencing," Grant went on. "It was everyday stuff like cars going by, light reflecting off those crystals, or branches moving in the wind."

"And the high EMF from the breaker box in the basement." Lyssa spoke up.

"That's right," Jason said. "I told Mr. and Mrs. Briscoe to have the box repaired. They should feel better once that gets taken care of."

"So that leaves us with just one area we still can't account for, right?" Lyssa went on.

"Right," Mike said. "The pennies."

"So what do we tell the Briscoes?" Lyssa asked.

"Nothing just yet," Grant replied. "The pennies are a clue. What do they mean? Do they belong to a spirit? What does the spirit want? We've got to find out about the pennies."

"Maybe the answer has to do with the people who lived in the house before the Briscoes," Jason told the team. He gave Mark Hammond a quick slap on the back. "Mark, that means you're up. It's time for you to do some of your research magic!"

Late that night, Mark was still at work at his desk. The rest of the team had gone home, even Mike. But Mark didn't want to leave yet. Not until he solved the puzzle.

Who was leaving the pennies in Scott and Jerry's room?

Why only seven pennies?

· Why the same arrangement, time after time?

Mark was sure the history of the house held the answers. His fingers tapped quickly on the laptop keyboard. He found out that the house was built in 1925.

Good news and bad news, Mark thought. From 1925 to the present is a pretty long time. He stared at the jar of pennies sitting on the table beside him. Jerry and Scott had let the team take the pennies back to the office to help with the investigation.

Mark unscrewed the jar lid and dumped the pennies out. He stared at them. *Do they hold a clue?*

He turned all the pennies heads up. Then he placed them in a line. He took a magnifying glass from his desk drawer and looked at the pennies super close up.

"Now we're getting somewhere," he said.

All the pennies were from between the years 1955 and 1967. *That has to be important,* he thought. *Why those years?*

Mark went back to the website on his laptop. About ten minutes later, he thought he had the answer.

Now all he had to do was wait till tomorrow. Then he could tell the others.

"All the pennies come from the same time period," he explained the next morning. The team gathered around the long table the Hammond brothers shared as a workstation. They looked at the pennies, which Mark had lined up in date order.

"From 1955 to 1967," he went on.

"Twelve years," Grant said.

"That's right," Mark said. "During that time, two families lived in the house. One for five years and the other for seven."

"Seven," Jason echoed.

Mark nodded. "I focused on the second family, because the number seven seemed important."

"What did you find out?" Lyssa asked.

"From 1960 to 1967, the house was owned by a family named—" Mark paused. But his hands were busy moving seven of the pennies into the same shape the boys always found in their bedroom. "A family named *Flowers*. Parents were Stan and Jessica. And one son, Daniel, who died in 1967. He was twelve years old."

"Did he die in the house?" Jason asked.

"No," Mark answered. "But he did die nearby. He was riding his bike along the road and got hit by a car."

"So there's a pretty good chance Daniel's room is now Scott and Jerry's," Mike said.

"I think so," Mark agreed.

"He might be trying to contact them," Grant said.

"But why leave pennies?" Lyssa asked.

Grant shook his head. "We'll probably never know. But it's time to tell the Briscoes what we *do* know."

"Right," Jason said. "Lyssa, you talked to the family first. I think you should make the call."

"Thank you for coming back," Janet Briscoe said. "The boys really appreciate it. My husband and I do too."

"We're happy to be here," Lyssa said. "I can't wait to see the surprise you said you have for us."

Lyssa had explained the team's theory about Daniel Flowers several days before. The family thanked them, and Lyssa mailed back the pennies in their jam jar. Then, just yesterday, Janet Briscoe had called. Scott and Jerry had something they wanted to show the team.

"Come see what we did!" Scott said as soon as he saw Jason and Grant.

"Yeah," Jerry said. "Come on. It's really cool. You're going to like it."

"Okay," Jason said. "Lead the way."

The two boys dashed up the stairs, heading for their bedroom. The grown-ups trailed along behind.

"It's over by the window," Scott said as the group entered the boys' bedroom. "Hurry up. Come on."

Lyssa noticed that the crystals were gone and the jam jar stood on the windowsill. On one side of the jar stood Jerry's Anakin Skywalker action figure. A Spock action figure stood on the other side.

"We made a spot for Daniel's pennies," Jerry said. "Then we added some of our favorite stuff. Because, you know."

"We thought maybe Daniel might like them," Scott explained. "It's sort of his room too, right? And, I mean, he never even got to see *any* of this."

Lyssa smiled. Trying to imagine a world without *Star Trek* or *Star Wars* was hard!

"Have there been any more pennies?" Grant asked.

Scott shook his head. "No. But that's okay too, because…" He paused, as if he wasn't quite sure what to say next. "Because it is, that's why."

"I think so too," Grant said. "What about you, Jay?"

"Me too." Jason nodded.

"Mom made chocolate chip cookies," Jerry said. "You guys want some?"

"Absolutely," Jason said.

"Race you!" Scott cried.

He darted around Grant and Jason and out the bedroom door.

"No fair!" Jerry shouted. "You didn't say ready, set, go!"

"I've been thinking about the Briscoe case," Lyssa said a couple of days later. Lyssa, Jason, and Grant were the only ones in the office. Everyone else had gone home for the day.

"Good work writing up the case notes," Jason said. "How does it feel? Your first case?"

"It feels good," Lyssa said. "And working with the team is awesome. I know I still have a lot to learn, though."

"Jay and I feel that way all the time," Grant said with a smile.

"I've been thinking about Daniel Flowers," Lyssa said. "If it *was* Daniel leaving those pennies, I think I understand why he stopped. I think he got what he wanted."

"What was that?" Jason asked.

"Friends," Lyssa said.

Grant and Jason smiled.

GHOST ON THE WATER

*W*hat was that?

Diana Martin sat straight up in her bunk on her family's houseboat.

Ba BOOM. Ba BOOM. Ba BOOM. Her heart pounded. Usually, Diana was a sound sleeper. Her mom always said Diana slept like a rock.

Not tonight.

Tonight, something jolted Diana so wide awake that she knew she couldn't go back to sleep.

Diana tossed back her covers and got out of bed. She stood for a moment, letting her legs adjust to the motion of the boat. The boat rocked gently from side to side.

The water was calm. Diana liked the calm nights. When a storm came in, things could really rock and roll.

She crossed to the door of her cabin. The cabin was so small that it took only two strides. She carefully stepped over the high threshold and out into the narrow hall.

Diana was twelve. She looked forward to vacation on her family's houseboat every summer. Her dad piloted the boat wherever they wanted to go. They would put all the places they liked into a hat and then draw them out one by one.

At least, that's what they used to do, but that changed when Mr. Martin discovered Heron's Point Dock, on a small island off the coast of Rhode Island. Heron's Point was her dad's favorite kind of place; it had one old wooden dock and nothing else. No tourist attractions. No crowds.

From their very first visit, Diana didn't like Heron's Point. She thought it was boring. And now... now she found it frightening.

At Heron's Point, Diana heard things. And saw things. And some of her things were moved or taken. Weird stuff happened every time the family tied up the boat there.

Her dad said the strange noises were harmless. He accused Diana of forgetting where she put things, then claiming someone moved them, but Diana knew the truth. Something was going on—she just couldn't explain it. Not yet anyhow.

Maybe she could find out tonight.

She reached the starboard steps that went from the sleeping

cabins belowdecks to the main cabin above. She listened for a moment to the gentle, lapping water.

Then she gripped the handrail tightly and started up. There weren't that many steps, but they were steep and narrow. It was easy to trip and fall.

Slowly, carefully, Diana poked her head up into the main cabin. The white deck gleamed almost as bright as in daylight. *Full moon,* Diana noticed.

Her eyes darted around the boat. Trying to see as much of it as possible. "All clear," she murmured to herself.

Maybe it was a false alarm. Maybe a raccoon had jumped on the dock. Raccoons were big and fat. They could make a lot of noise. Enough noise to wake her up.

Bam! Bam!

Diana gasped in surprise and her foot slipped off the step.

BAM BAM BAM!

"Ohhh!" she cried out as her head bashed hard against the wall. Pain shot down her body. She clamped her eyes shut, trying to force the pain away.

She held on to the railing. Felt the boat rock from side to side. Slowly she opened her eyes.

There's something here! she realized.

Something on the other side of the boat.

An intruder.

NOT a raccoon.

But who is it? WHAT is it?

Diana opened her mouth to call her father. But then she stopped herself. He never believed her stories. She had to get proof on her own. She fought back her fear, took a deep breath, and climbed onto the swaying deck. Staying low, she slithered across the main cabin on her belly like a snake.

The main cabin was the family living room. There were big windows on all sides. It made looking out easy. But it made looking *in* easy too.

Don't think about that now, she told herself.

Keeping down, Diana reached the starboard side of the cabin. She was as close to the dock as she could get and still be inside the boat. She was breathing in short, fast gasps. She felt as if she had been running a race. Her head still throbbed from her fall. She was determined to ignore it. This time she was going to solve the mystery of Heron's Point.

Diana climbed to her hands and knees and peered out. The full moon made the world outside nearly as bright as day. But the color had all been drained away. And the bluish black shadows were long and creepy.

Nothing looks real, Diana thought. *It's like I'm dreaming.*

She could see the wooden dock beside the boat. She could see the moonlight sparkling on the water. Diana stuck her head up a little more.

She squinted through the window—

—and her heart stopped.

She wasn't alone.

Someone was on the dock. Covered in shadow. She saw him only a few feet from her face.

He was staring right at her.

Diana opened her mouth to scream. She couldn't make a sound. She froze. It was as if her entire body had turned to stone.

She stared at the man. He was dressed in the kind of old clothes her dad wore when they went out in bad weather.

Who is he? How did he get here? Where's his boat?

Does he live on the island?

What does he WANT?

The figure moved. A strangled sound escaped Diana's throat. She blinked. She didn't believe what she was seeing.

The man didn't walk. His feet didn't move. He seemed to *glide*.

He moved to the edge of the dock. Close enough for Diana to see clearly.

He wasn't standing *on* the dock. He was *above* it. Hovering in the air. Floating over the edge.

"Go away," Diana murmured. Her voice came out in a choked whisper. "Please—go away. Leave us alone." To her surprise, the floating figure fell back.

"Go away!" Diana repeated. Her voice came out a little stronger this time.

She pulled herself up from her hands and knees. Stood as tall as she could. "Did you hear me? Go away and leave us alone!"

The man began to sway from side to side. As if he wanted to go somewhere but couldn't decide which direction to take.

"Go *away!*" Diana screamed. "Go away!"

The floating man vanished. Like smoke.

Diana still stared at the gray dock.

Just shadows now. Shadows and moonlight.

Her knees started to shake. She reached out for the nearest chair and dropped into it. With a deep, shuddering breath, she pulled her knees up to her chin and wrapped her arms around her legs. She rocked from side to side.

"Don't come back," she whispered. "Go away. Go away and leave us alone." Over and over. Rock, rock. Back and forth. From side to side. "Don't come back. Go away. Go away and leave us alone."

That's how her parents found her the next morning.

At least this time they believed her.

They believed her when she said she had seen a ghost.

"I have to ask," Jen said. "Have we *ever* done anything like this before?"

Jen's question made Lyssa shiver. The TAPS teammates plus

Jason and Grant were in a small powerboat. They were on their way to Heron's Point Dock to investigate a haunted houseboat.

"Nope," Jason answered. "It's pretty much a TAPS first."

He tucked one hand into his jacket pocket. He held on to the side of the boat with the other.

The sun was lowering in front of them. It made the water sparkle with red and gold. The air felt chilly. The water had choppy waves. The small boat bounced up and down, like a carnival thrill ride.

Lyssa held on tight. She felt excited. Jen was right. How many times did you get to investigate the possibility of a haunted boat?

"Do the Martins live on the houseboat year-round?" she asked.

"No," Grant answered. "They mainly use it in the summer for vacations. It's big enough to live on, but Diana, the twelve-year-old daughter, has to go to school."

"She's the one who has made most of the claims, right?" Jen asked.

"Yes," Grant answered. "She says she's seen a full-bodied apparition."

"I don't know about you guys," Jason said. "But I can't wait to get started. Heron's Point is a very old, very lonely spot. The perfect place for paranormal activity."

"I'm excited too," Lyssa agreed. "I mean, a haunted house-boat? How cool is that?" The boat bounced hard. Frothy water splashed over the side. Lyssa dodged away from it.

"Look!" Grant said. He pointed. "I think we're almost there."

Up ahead, Lyssa could see a small island. It looked like a green hill growing out of the ocean.

As they roared closer, she could see that the island was mostly covered with trees. She could make out a rocky shoreline and a half-moon cove dead ahead.

Jason pointed to a long wooden dock on the right side of the cove. A single boat was tied up beside the dock.

"Wow!" Jen said. "That is a big boat!"

"It looks huge from here," Grant said. "But you'll be surprised at how small it feels inside. Good thing we left the twins back at the office."

The Hammond brothers—Mike and Mark—had agreed to stay behind. They would go to work on the case after the evidence was collected.

"Get ready, everyone," Jason said. He glanced up at the sky. "There's a storm coming in. Take a look at those clouds. Something tells me we're in for a rocky night."

The three Martins welcomed the TAPS team onto the boat.

Lyssa took a few awkward steps across the deck. She knew it would take a while to get her sea legs.

She couldn't stop staring. The houseboat was just awesome. On the outside, the boat looked like a big, tall speedboat.

The decks were polished wood. There were metal handrails all around the deck. They were so shiny, Lyssa could see her reflection. A short gangplank led from the dock to the boat itself.

Hey! I just walked the plank, Lyssa thought with a smile.

"Thank you for coming," Mr. Martin said. He led the way into what looked exactly like a normal living room. There was a couch, a coffee table, a couple of chairs. There was even a rug. Big windows on three sides reflected the red setting sun. The only things that felt unusual were the super-low ceilings.

At the front of the boat, Lyssa caught a glimpse of the pilot's station. There were tons of navigation equipment, a radio, and some round video screens.

Just to her left, she saw a short, steep flight of steps with handrails on both sides.

That must lead to the sleeping cabins and the galley, she thought.

Mr. Martin sat down on the couch. He gestured for everyone else to sit down, and then his expression turned serious. "I want to get to the bottom of this as soon as possible," he said, and glanced at Diana, sitting shyly beside him on the couch.

He's not very happy to see us, Lyssa thought. Jason said the dad had more trouble believing what his daughter said.

"How quickly can it be done?" Mr. Martin asked. "I don't want this to drag on. I mean, this is our vacation."

Grant leaned forward in his chair. He scratched his ear. "We'll

47

do our best," he promised. "We can't really promise a timeline. Let's see what happens tonight. Then we'll get in touch."

Mr. Martin nodded. "Sounds good."

Lyssa turned to Diana. She liked the girl's wavy dark hair and bright green eyes. But Diana looked pale and troubled.

"So," she said to Diana. "Do you like to vacation on the boat every summer?"

"Usually, I do," Diana said. She tugged nervously at a strand of hair. "We used to go all over. But lately…" Her voice trailed off.

"What Diana is trying to say is that lately we've been coming only to Heron's Point," Mr. Martin spoke up. "Diana would like a shopping mall everywhere we go. I prefer to get away from the crowds."

Mrs. Martin smiled. "He's been very stubborn. He really likes it here."

"The report you gave us was very clear," Lyssa said to Diana. "Lots of good details. You gave us a lot to go on."

"Good," Diana said quietly. She kept her eyes down. "I… wanted to help. It was…pretty scary."

"Diana hasn't been able to sleep at night," her mother said.

"I keep picturing that creepy man," Diana said. "Floating. He…he was so close to me." She shuddered.

Mr. Martin put an arm around her shoulders. "Let's leave the boat to them now. Okay, Diana? I'm sure they'll have an answer for you."

"We'll see what we can find," Grant said.

Mr. Martin jumped to his feet. He pulled Diana up. "We better get going. The wind is really picking up."

"Ready whenever you are," Mrs. Martin said.

The family was going back to the mainland. They were taking the same boat that brought the TAPS team out to Heron's Point. A friend of theirs was the pilot.

Then we'll be all alone out here, Lyssa realized. She gazed out the window. The sun was nearly down. The water had darkened to a charcoal color. *Just us and the boat bobbing on the water in the dark...with a ghost on board?*

"We'll be in touch tomorrow, then," Mr. Martin said. "Come on, you two. Let's go."

They swung backpacks over their shoulders. Mrs. Martin had a small suitcase. They made their way onto the dock. Lyssa watched them climb into the small motorboat. A few minutes later, they roared off.

"Okay," Jason said. "Let's get the equipment set up. It will be dark before we know it."

"One good thing about the close quarters," Jen said. She opened a trunk and began to unpack. "Anything moves or makes a sound? The equipment should pick it right up."

"Outstanding," Grant said. "Let's get on it. Let's see if we can find that floating old man in the raggedy clothes."

Soon after dark, the storm hit hard. Heavy rains drummed the deck, sending up a roar. The wind howled. The boat rocked and bumped against the dock.

"Lyssa? You feeling okay?" Lyssa felt Jason's hand on her shoulder.

"Why? Is my face green?" Lyssa replied.

"It's too dark to tell," Jason said.

The boat lurched up, then down. Lyssa's stomach rose and fell with each toss of the waves.

Despite the storm, they had all worked hard. The equipment was set to go.

"I do feel a little woozy," Lyssa admitted. "All this tilting up and down. It's weird. The longer we're here, the smaller everything feels."

"Yeah, it's like the cabin walls are closing in on us," Jen chimed in. "I swear, I bump into something every time I turn around."

"Tell you what," Jason said. "Jen and Lyssa, you take this level. Grant and I will investigate down below."

"Really? Sounds good." Lyssa sighed. She felt relieved. But she knew Jason didn't like small spaces any more than she did. "You're sure?"

"No worries," Jason said.

"Everybody ready?" Grant poked his head up from the stairs.

"Oh, yeah," Lyssa said. "Ready to rock and roll."

"Okay, then," Jason said. "Let's go dark."

Going dark on a boat really is *going dark*, Lyssa thought.

She and Jen stood still, waiting for their eyes to adjust. There were some colored lights on the navigation equipment—small red and green lights. But other than that it was total blackness. No streetlights or lights from passing cars. No chance of a nightlight or two down a hall. No moonlight or starlight. The sky was covered by heavy, black storm clouds.

The boat's motion felt bigger in the dark. Sounds grew louder. The wind moaned. The water went *slap, slap, slap,* trapped between the boat and the dock. The boat creaked and groaned, rolling on the sharp, steady waves.

And all around them was deep, dark water.

Lyssa shivered. Even with Jen close by, she felt alone on this small bobbing boat. A tiny speck compared to all this water.

She took a deep breath and shoved these thoughts away. After all, she had a job to do.

"This is Lyssa. I'm in the main cabin with Jen," she said out loud for the recorder.

"I want to take an EMF reading," Jen said. "With all this equipment, I expect the magnetic field to be fairly high. I don't want us to get fooled and think it's paranormal." She moved toward the navigation equipment in the front of the boat.

Lyssa stayed toward the back. "What's the reading?" she called. She had to shout over the howling wind outside.

"Like I thought. It's pretty high, over five," Jen called back.

"Makes sense," Lyssa said. "Even so. A high level in a small space like this could add to the general creep factor."

"Definitely," Jen agreed. "Did Diana say she went outside onto the dock?"

"Nope," Lyssa said. "She said she stayed inside."

"Well, maybe the high EMF—" Jen started. But she stopped suddenly. "Hey!"

"What is it?" Lyssa asked. "What's wrong?"

She began to move toward Jen. She took two steps. The boat jerked up, up, up. With a startled cry, Lyssa lurched to one side and crashed into the side of the couch.

"Whoa. I thought I saw something," Jen called in a trembling voice. "Outside. On the dock."

Lyssa struggled to her feet. She staggered to the window. She pressed her face against the glass. The glass felt icy cold.

"I—I can't see anything," she stammered. "What did you see out there?"

Lyssa couldn't make out Jen's reply. "What?" she called. "I can't hear you."

Jen appeared at Lyssa's side. Lyssa jumped. Her forehead smacked against the hard window glass.

"Ouch!" she cried. "I'm getting beat up here!"

"Are you okay?" Jen asked.

"Guess I don't have my sea legs," Lyssa said, rubbing her sore forehead. "And I couldn't hear you, Jen. Why were you whispering?"

"Huh? Whispering? I didn't whisper," Jen said.

"I...I heard you whisper something," Lyssa insisted. "But—" She stopped.

She heard it again. Another whisper.

Right behind her.

Jen's mouth dropped open in shock. Her eyes went wide as she turned to Lyssa.

Jen heard it too.

A hoarse whisper. So close in the tiny, dark cabin.

Jen and Lyssa spun around. Lyssa fumbled for the switch on her flashlight and clicked it on. Bright light stabbed through the cabin of the houseboat. It caught the glass of the big window opposite where she and Jen stood.

"Turn it off. Turn it off!" Jen cried. "You'll scare it away."

Lyssa cut off the flashlight. "Sorry. It was so close. You heard that, right? Tell me you heard that."

"I heard it," Jen said. "It was right behind us. I couldn't make out any words, though. Could you?"

"No, I couldn't. Let me see if I can make contact." Lyssa took a deep, shuddering breath. "Is there anybody here?" she asked quietly, calmly. "I'm Lyssa and this is Jen. Is there someone else here with us?"

As if answering her, the houseboat lurched back and forth. Lyssa grabbed onto Jen. They both struggled to keep their balance.

"Weird. Why is the boat rocking so hard?" Lyssa asked.

"I don't know," Jen said. "I think we have to go out there and find out."

"I *knew* you were going to say that," Lyssa said.

Jen was quiet for a moment. Finally, she whispered, "We're Ghost Hunters. We can do this, right?"

"Right. You go first."

Jen opened the door. Cold air poured into the houseboat. "Don't trip," she warned before stepping out onto the outside deck. Lyssa followed. The rain had stopped, but Lyssa felt the force of the wind at once. It felt like giant hands trying to pluck the two TAPS team members right off the boat.

"Lyssa." Jen spun around to face her. "Check this out."

She held up her EMF meter. "It went all the way to over ten," she said. "That's a huge jump. It could mean something is here."

"I don't see anything, do you?" Lyssa asked.

"No," Jen answered.

Bam. Bam. BAM BAM BAM!

The boat slammed into the dock. Only the outside railing kept Lyssa and Jen from tumbling overboard.

Jen shivered. "Maybe we should go back inside and wait for the wind to die down a bit. What do you think?"

Lyssa opened her mouth to answer, but no sound came out. As the winds howled around her, she stared straight ahead. Stared without blinking…without breathing.

Stared at the figure on the dock.

The man who was staring back at her.

As Lyssa stood frozen on the deck, everything went still and silent. She couldn't hear the wind. She couldn't feel the rocking and tossing of the boat.

She could only stare at the figure at the far end of the dock. A man…in ragged old clothes.

"Are you seeing this? Please tell me you're seeing this," she breathed to Jen.

"Yes," Jen whispered back. "I see him."

His face was lost behind shadows. But Lyssa could feel his eyes on her. She knew he was staring back at her.

He wore a cap. It looked like a Navy captain's cap. She could clearly see the outlines of his large overcoat. The hem ragged and torn, falling over baggy trousers.

She sucked in a breath as the man started to move. Slowly he moved along the dock. Gliding closer.

Lyssa whispered, "He's not walking. Look, Jen—he's floating. Off the dock."

Closer.

I am looking at a real live ghost, Lyssa thought.

For the first time, face-to-face with a ghost.

What if he gets angry? What if he doesn't want us here?

She gazed around, feeling panic. Nowhere to run. Nowhere to hide.

And then suddenly, the apparition stopped moving. It hovered in the air just inches off the dock.

This man... he's just as Diana described, Lyssa thought.

The figure became hazy. The storm winds seemed to blow him apart. Then he shimmered back together.

He's dressed for sailing, Lyssa saw. And yes, that was a Navy cap on his head.

Make contact, Lyssa, she told herself. *Do your job!*

"Um. Hello," she called. "I'm Lyssa and this is Jen. Can you hear us?"

"We want to know who you are," Jen spoke up. "Is there something you want to tell us? Something we can do to help you?"

The figure shimmered and faded. The wind seemed to blow him away. Then he reappeared, rippling, shaking.

"Is there a reason you return here?" Lyssa asked. "Is there something we should know about you or about this place?"

Lyssa gasped as the ghostly figure rose into the air. It floated above her. It swayed from side to side. Like a kite carried by a strong breeze.

Lyssa took a step back. But there was nowhere to go. No way

to escape from the spirit. Fear gripped her. She wanted to scream, but no sound came. She stood and waited for the ghost to board the boat…

Then he vanished.

Gone.

The sky was black. The dock empty. The wind howled all around.

Lyssa hugged herself tightly. But she couldn't stop shivering. "Let's g-go get J-Jason and Grant," she stammered.

She let Jen lead her back into the cabin.

Out of the wind, she shut her eyes. But she still saw the ghost in front of her. Floating. Shadowy. And totally real!

"Let's go over it again," Grant said.

It was a few days later. The TAPS team was in the conference room back in their office.

Lyssa was glad to be back on land. But the excitement of the case hadn't faded.

"Well, we had quite a bit of paranormal activity on this one," Grant began. "The voice Lyssa and Jen heard comes through very clearly on the audio."

"And Lyssa and Jen also had a sighting," Jason added. "Unfortunately that was out of the range of the video camera. But they both saw the same apparition."

Mike and his twin, Mark, stared at Lyssa and Jen. "How does it feel?" Mark asked.

"I can tell you how it *felt*," Lyssa said. "I was absolutely terrified. It was like every shred of training went right out of my head."

"The two of us…" Jen started. "It took us a while. Staring at that guy. But we finally got ourselves together. We tried to communicate with him."

"But he sailed off with the wind," Lyssa said. She motioned with one hand. "Poof."

"Well, at least we can tell Mr. Martin that his daughter didn't make the whole thing up," Mike said.

"Actually," Mark started. He flipped open a folder and pulled out several pieces of paper. "We can do better than that."

The next day, Jason, Lyssa, and Mark returned to the Martins' houseboat. It was a warm, sunny day. The storm clouds had moved on.

"We think we have some explanations for what your daughter experienced," Jason told Diana's parents.

"Not only that," he continued, "Lyssa and her teammate Jen saw a figure of a man."

Diana's face filled with surprise. "You saw *him*? For real?"

"For real," Lyssa said. "I'm going to remember it for the rest of my life."

"Wow." Diana turned to her dad. "So now we know I'm not going nuts!"

"Honey, I never thought you were going nuts," her father said. "I just couldn't understand."

"Well, maybe this will help," Mark began. "While these guys were investigating here on the boat, I did some research about Heron's Point. This whole island was private property until just a couple of years ago."

"Somebody owned the whole island?" Diana said.

Mark nodded. "The man who owned this island was named Peter Stone. He lived on a houseboat—something like this one. Until there was a tragedy. One day his boat caught fire, and he was trapped inside."

"Did he die?" Diana asked. "Did he die in the fire?"

"Yes, he did," Mark answered softly. "Right here at Heron's Point Dock. We think the spirit you saw may be Peter Stone."

"What about all the other things Diana told us about?" Mr. Martin asked. "The banging noises and stuff showing up in strange places?"

"The banging noise has a more everyday explanation," Jason said. "It's the bumpers on the dock. They're old and loose. They make a lot of noise when your boat hits them just right."

"Well," Mr. Martin said. "So at least the bumpers aren't haunted."

"We *never* assume anything is haunted," Jason said. "We always come with an open mind. And we actually *like* to debunk things. It makes the times when we do decide we've encountered the paranormal that much stronger. I'd like to play a recording for you."

He turned to Lyssa. "Please play back the recording you made in the main cabin."

"Will do," Lyssa said. She pulled out the portable recorder. The sound was already cued up. She pressed the play button.

Everyone listened.

"I can hear footsteps. Is that you?" Diana asked.

"Yes." Lyssa nodded.

Then the whisper came on. So clear and close by that even Mr. Martin jumped.

After the whisper—just silence. Lyssa turned off the equipment.

"I wish we could tell you we know what the voice says," Jason said. "We can't make out the words. But the voice certainly sounds like a human whisper. It's a very clear recording…"

"A recording of a ghost?" Mr. Martin asked.

Jason nodded.

"Hey, check it out," Lyssa said a couple of weeks later. "We just got a letter from Diana Martin."

"What does it say?" Jen asked.

Lyssa opened the envelope.

"Dear Jason, Grant, and all the TAPS team," she read aloud. *"Thank you for coming to our houseboat. You helped us a lot! Even my dad thinks so."*

"I'm glad to hear that," Grant said with a smile.

"We had a family meeting after you left. We decided to do some work at Heron's Point. Dad made some repairs to the dock. He replaced some rotting timbers. And he took off the old bumpers and put on brand-new ones. Guess what? The banging sound is gone.

"But here's the best part. I haven't seen the Heron's Point ghost again. Mom says she thinks maybe Peter Stone was trying to warn us. But things are safer now that we fixed up the dock. So he doesn't have to hang around.

"True confession: I still don't always find my stuff where I thought I put it. But I guess Dad was right about this one thing at least. It's probably me and not a ghost.

"Thank you so much for helping our family. Now I like going to Heron's Point. Anytime you want to sail with us, just give a call. I promise it won't be scary.

"Yours sincerely,
Diana Martin."

GHOSTS
WITH
NO
LEGS

Bill Turner was scared. Big-time scared.

It was midnight. He was supposed to be in bed. But here he was. Creeping downstairs in the dark house, his back pressed tight against the wall. He wished he could make himself flat as a pancake, or maybe even flatter. That way, he wouldn't stick out into the hall.

Because Bill didn't want to stick out. Not when there might be something in the hall, something he didn't want to get too close to.

What was that?

Bill froze. His right foot hovered over the fourth step from the bottom. His heart pounded. His ears strained for the slightest sound.

Nothing. There's nothing there, he thought. *Just keep going.*

He had to make it all the way downstairs. He had to make it to his secret place. His safe place. Then he could put his plan into action.

Somebody had to do *something* about what was going on in his house. Mom and Dad sure hadn't come through so far. Bill's older brother, David, was no help at all. Dave was fifteen. He pretended Bill didn't exist. Mindy, their little sister, was only seven. Too little.

That just leaves me, Bill thought.

He put his foot down.

Creeaak.

That step always creaked if he put his foot down wrong. Cold sweat trickled down the back of Bill's neck. The best place to put his foot was in the very middle of the step.

To do that, he had to move away from the wall.

Please don't come, he prayed. *Please don't come tonight. At least not until I get all the way down the stairs.*

Bill held his breath. Stretched out his leg. And put his foot down.

Aaaarrrr.

The house gave an unearthly groan.

Bill raced down the last four steps. He didn't care if he made any noise. He dropped to his knees at the bottom of the stairs. His fingers fumbled in the dark, searching for the knob on the door to his secret place: a tiny room underneath the stairs.

Got it!

He pulled open the door and crawled forward on his hands and knees. He twisted sideways. He barely fit. But he could squeeze in. He had to.

Bill reached out and closed the door.

Darkness. Black. Complete. Total.

Bill squished himself into a sitting position. His neck was twisted. But at least he didn't hit his head like last night.

That was when he had hidden the flashlight and his other supplies. They were in the deepest, darkest corner of his hiding place. But Bill didn't reach for the flashlight. Not yet. He didn't want to turn it on. Not until he was sure it was safe.

Suddenly he felt it coming. *The cold.* A cold so fierce it made his stomach muscles quiver. Bill's lungs burned. It was like he was breathing solid ice.

He bit down on his tongue. Otherwise, his teeth would start chattering. The noise might give him away.

He listened, but he heard nothing. No sound. No clue. No warning. But he *knew*. Bill knew he was no longer alone.

Outside his hiding place, there was a man. A man that only Bill could see. A man who shouldn't be there at all.

But he *was* there. Night after night. Always at the same time. The man came up the stairs. He went past Dave's room. Past Mindy's room. On and on and on, straight toward Bill's room. Straight toward Bill.

And there was nothing Bill could do to stop him.

Then every night the man vanished while standing right inside Bill's bedroom door. Like a puff of smoke. The man was there one minute, gone the next.

Because of the nightly visitor, Bill couldn't sleep. He nodded off at his desk during school. His homeroom teacher called his mom. Then Mom asked if he wanted to sleep in Dave's room, and Bill realized the truth—Mom was scared too. She knew there was something wrong in their house. She just didn't know what to do about it.

But Bill did. He had a plan.

Bill felt something change that he couldn't describe. He realized he was breathing easier. It wasn't so cold anymore. The man was past and on his way up the stairs. On his way to Bill's empty bedroom.

Now! Bill thought.

He stretched out his arm. His fingers found the flashlight. They wrapped around it. His thumb found the switch and turned it on.

After the total dark, the small flashlight beam seemed bright as the sun. Bill blinked his eyes. Then, quickly, he found the rest of the things he had hidden. Paper. Pen. Envelopes and stamps.

He set the flashlight on the floor and leaned over the paper. He uncapped the pen.

This has got to work, he thought. *It's just got to.*

Dear Ghost Hunters,

he wrote.

Please help us.

"Okay," Jason said. He stretched. "Great follow-up meeting, guys. All our cases are wrapped. That doesn't happen very often. Maybe it's time for a vacation."

"Not so fast," TAPS researcher Mark Hammond said. He had to raise his voice. Everybody else in the room was laughing.

"Uh-oh," Mark's twin brother, Mike, said. "Somebody pushed Mark's serious button."

Mark smiled at his brother. "I think this could be *very* serious," he said. He opened a big envelope and pulled out several sheets of paper. "Bill Turner thinks so anyway."

"Who's Bill Turner?" Grant asked.

"He's the kid who wrote this."

Mark picked up the top sheet of paper. He held it out so the others could see.

Grant looked at the letter. "Why don't you read it to us?" he suggested.

"Yeah," Mike said. "But no funny voices."

"Nothing about this is funny," Mark said. He gripped the papers tightly. "Trust me."

Dear Ghost Hunters,

Please help us.

At night. That's when the man comes. But not every night. That would actually be better.

That sounds weird, doesn't it?

But it's true. When something happens all the time, you can get ready for it. Even if it's something you don't like. But you can't be ready all the time.

I can't, anyhow.

My older brother—his name is Dave—would say that makes me a wimp. I say, it makes me normal.

I should probably back up, huh?

My name is Bill Turner. I'm twelve years old. I live in Peekskill,

New York. My parents are named Steve and Dana. I have a younger sister named Mindy. She's seven. I already told you about Dave. He's fifteen and thinks he knows everything. So, really, the less said about him, the better.

We used to live in California. Then Dad got transferred to New York. So we moved. Our house is big. It's pretty new. That's what Mom likes best about it. It has two floors, plus a basement and an attic. What I like best is I got to pick my own room. It's a great big one at the end of the upstairs hall.

At first, we were happy here. We all thought the new house was cool. Then the bad stuff started. The stuff I can't explain. That I can't tell anyone. But I know the truth.

Our new house is haunted.

That's why I'm writing to you.

It all started a month ago on January 5. I know because I put a big black X on my calendar. I watch your show all the time. I know you have to write stuff down. To document it. So that's what I did. I even have my own case file. I put it in the envelope along with this letter. So you can see I'm serious about this.

It started the night I heard my parents arguing.

My parents don't fight. Well, hardly ever. I can't explain it. They just always get along. Dave says it's weird. He says parents are supposed to fight. But I say Dave is full of it. Just because he can't get along with anyone...

71

So what happened was, I got up late at night. I wanted a drink of water. Usually, I keep a water bottle right by my bed. But that night I forgot to fill it up. So I grabbed the bottle and I headed downstairs to the kitchen. That's when I heard my parents arguing.

"What do you mean we shouldn't tell the kids?" my mother said. "Of course we should tell them."

"Honey, you're being emotional about this," my dad said.

"Emotional!" My mom's voice went up like when Mindy plays scales on the piano. And it got a whole lot louder. "Of course I'm being emotional!"

My dad made a shushing noise.

"They're our children, Steve," Mom went on in a quieter voice. "It's our job to protect them."

"From what?" my father asked. "What, precisely, do you think we should tell them?"

Uh-oh, I thought.

Precisely is one of my dad's favorite words. But he only brings it out on special occasions. Like, say, when he's absolutely, positively sure he's right. Precisely is the way my dad wins the few fights my parents actually have.

There was this really long silence.

"I don't know," my mother said. Her voice sounded tired. "I just don't know, Steve."

"There," Dad said, "that's my point. Until we know what we're up against here, we should keep the kids in the dark."

"In the dark," my mother echoed.

"You know what I mean, Dana," my father said. His voice was impatient now.

"Yes," my mother answered. "I know. But you're forgetting something, aren't you?"

"What's that?"

"In the dark...That's where those things hide."

Mark paused and looked up from the letter.

"Okay, now I'm starting to get scared," Lyssa said with a shudder. "Is that all?"

"No way," Mark said. "There's a whole lot more. Listen. I'll read the rest."

The dark...where those things hide.

That's what my mom said. I could have done without over-hearing that, let me tell you.

I heard my parents' footsteps. Any minute, they would come out of the living room. They would spot me in the downstairs hall.

I sprinted for the kitchen, careful to run on the balls of

my feet. That way, I wouldn't make any noise. I crouched behind the kitchen table. All the chairs were pushed in. Even if Mom and Dad looked into the kitchen, they wouldn't be able to see me at all.

But they didn't look. Mom and Dad went upstairs. They turned off the lights. Now I was all alone in the dark.

Where those things hide.

Why did Mom say that? I wondered. What did she mean by "those things"?

I'm not just some kid who's scared of the dark. Though I am. Kind of. Don't tell anyone.

I filled up the water bottle and headed back upstairs. I was halfway up when I felt the cold.

Most people think cold is just cold. You put on a sweater and it's no big deal. But this cold was something more. You know what I mean, right? You're Ghost Hunters, after all.

The cold came from nowhere. That was the first thing. Sure, it was January. But I was in the middle of the house. Not near a window or a door. One minute it was normal temperature. The next minute I can see my breath, like when I'm outside in the snow.

I spun around.

Nothing.

Of course it's nothing, Bill, I thought. Dave is right. You are a wimp.

Then why was my heart pounding so fast? So hard? My breath was making big white clouds as I breathed in and out. I kept on going toward my bedroom. Up the stairs. One by one. My teeth were chattering when I got to the top. I don't know what made me do it, but I turned around.

There was a man behind me at the bottom of the stairs. He was staring straight ahead. I don't think he saw me. I wanted to scream my head off. To yell for Mom and Dad.

Something stopped me. I can't explain. It's like there was this big fist in the middle of my throat. Choking me. Choking off even the possibility of sound.

I backed up.

Step. Step. Step.

The man began to climb the stairs. Coming toward me.

Step. Step. Step.

I was in my bedroom now.

Step. Step. Step.

The back of my knees bumped against my bed. I climbed up on it. But I didn't turn around. There was no way I was turning my back. I scooted all the way to the head of my bed.

There's nowhere else to go! I'm trapped!

I could see the man's head. Then his shoulders. And his chest. He kept on coming up the stairs! Coming straight toward me. He was in the hall now. Almost to my bedroom door. I could see his waist. But his legs...

His legs!

I did scream then. I couldn't stop myself.

All the way up the stairs he came. Along the hall to the door of my room.

Except he couldn't have. There was no way he could do that.

He didn't have any legs.

"Wow!" Jen Shorewood said. "That is so creepy." She shivered. "Just hearing about it makes *me* cold. So, we're going to help this kid, right?"

"This could be tricky," Grant said. "Officially, the family hasn't asked for any help. By which I mean the parents. We can't just show up."

"But there must be something we can do," Mark said. "We can't ignore what's going on."

"Bill's letter said he kept a case file," Jason said.

Mark nodded. "It's right here." He spread the papers out and looked them over quickly. "In addition to a stair-climbing guy, there's also a woman who walks around in the kitchen and a kid about Bill's little sister's age who runs back and forth—maybe she's playing or something—in the downstairs hall."

"Do any of the others have legs?" Mike asked. "And for the record, I can't believe I just asked that question."

"No," Mark said. "None of them. And here's something else. They do the same thing, over and over."

"That's interesting," Grant commented.

"At least let me do some research," Mark said. "Maybe if I can figure out who these ghosts are, I can solve the puzzle of what's going on. Then we could get in touch with the parents. When we have something solid to tell them."

"Sounds like a good approach," Jason said. "Keep us posted."

"Will do," Mark promised.

The meeting broke up. Mark put Bill's letter and case file back in the envelope. He tucked it under his arm.

His brother came to stand beside him. "You okay?" Mike asked.

"Yeah," Mark said. "Mostly. I just hate to think of that kid all on his own. We saw some pretty freaky stuff when we were kids."

"We did," Mike agreed. "But we got through it."

"I know. That's why I have to help him. Even if the team can't take the case. Even if I can't make the ghosts go away. I want Bill to know he's not alone in this. He's got solid backup."

The brothers fell silent. Both were thinking of their unusual childhood growing up in a haunted house.

"Well," Mike finally said. He poked Mark in the gut with his index finger. "After that burger and fries you had for lunch, I'd say you've got the *solid* part covered."

"You're the one who had the chocolate shake," Mark came right back. "Not to mention you ate most of my fries."

The brothers grinned at each other.

"You need any backup yourself, you let me know," Mike said.

"Thanks. I'll do that," Mark replied.

"Where are you going to start?" Mike asked.

"Easy," Mark said. "I'm going to go back in time."

"It's got to be here," Mark muttered several days later. He was working late at the office. Mark rubbed his eyes. He was tired. He felt as if he had been staring at the computer screen forever.

"Who are these ghosts?" he asked himself. "What are they doing in Bill's house? There's got to be an explanation. There's got to be *something* in the past."

He hadn't found it so far.

Mark stopped staring at the computer and stared at Bill's letter instead. He kept it right beside him on the desk. To remind him of why he shouldn't give up—why he should keep on going.

I'm not just some kid who's scared of the dark. Though I am. Kind of. Don't tell anyone.

That's what Bill had said. But Mark knew exactly what he meant.

Bill is more than scared, Mark thought. *Bill Turner is terrified. And it won't get any better—until I find a way to help him.*

Mark's gaze strayed to the stack of papers beside Bill's letter. The pile was enormous. Doing the research on where the Turners lived was actually sort of fun. Mark loved going back to the historical record. He loved finding answers in the past when the present stumped everyone else.

Trouble was, both past *and* present were stumping him now.

It wasn't that the ghosts kept doing the same thing over and over. Mark had seen cases like that before. Not very often, but there were quite a few in the TAPS files. There was one big difference in this case. The spirits in those hauntings had all their body parts.

Why don't the ghosts in Bill Turner's house have any legs? Mark wondered.

There had to be a reason. Mark was sure of it. So why couldn't he find one?

He pawed through the papers impatiently. Some tumbled off the table and fell to the floor. Mark ignored them.

"Come on," he muttered. "Come on, what's the answer?"

He pulled out a paper from the very bottom of the stack. *Go back to the beginning,* he thought. Mark began his search with an old map. It showed what the area where Bill Turner now lived used to look like. Once the whole area was farm country. One big farm, in fact. The original farmhouse stood in the same spot as Bill's house.

The farmhouse, Mark thought. He shuffled through the papers again. He pulled out a second map. This one showed the floor plan of the original farmhouse.

Mark ran his finger through the rooms, as if he were trying to find his way through a maze. Through the front door and into the downstairs hall. Then up a flight of stairs to the second floor.

If Bill lived in the old farmhouse, Mark thought, *his bedroom would be right at the end of the hall. Right* there.

Mark's finger froze. His heart began to pound. *Wait a minute. Wait just a minute here,* he thought.

He turned back to his computer. He typed in a command. A moment later, the web page for the housing development where Bill Turner lived appeared on the screen. Mark navigated through the website until he found what he wanted.

That's it! he thought. *That's it right there!*

The old farmhouse and Bill Turner's house looked exactly alike. The new house was bigger. But the layout was the same.

Excited now, Mark printed out what the website showed. Then he checked the time. It was 9:30 PM. Still okay. Mark's mom had this rule when the boys were growing up. No phone calls after ten o'clock. Even now that Mark was grown up, this rule still stuck.

Mark picked up the phone. His first phone call was to Jason.

"Hey, Jason. It's Mark," he said. "Good news on the Bill Turner case. I think I figured out what's going on."

"That's great news," Jason said. "Give me the rundown."

Quickly, Mark explained.

"That does make sense," Jason agreed when Mark was finished. "Really great job."

"I want to contact Bill's parents," Mark said. "Now that we have a possible answer, I think the time is right."

"I agree," Jason said. "Go for it. Let me know how it goes."

"Will do," Mark said.

He hung up. Then he pulled out Bill's letter. The Turner address and phone number were printed at the bottom of the page.

"Okay, Mr. and Mrs. Turner," Mark said to himself as he punched in the phone number. "Please don't freak out."

He listened to the phone ring. "Hello?" he said when a woman's voice answered the phone. "Is this Mrs. Turner?"

"Yes," the voice replied. She sounded puzzled. Mark couldn't blame her. He quickly explained.

"Mrs. Turner, my name is Mark Hammond," he said. "We've never met, but your son Bill wrote to me about a week ago. I work for TAPS, The Atlantic Paranormal Society. I've been doing some research.

"I think I know what's going on inside your house."

"Thank you for agreeing to meet with me," Mark said. "I know getting a call from a total stranger might seem, well, kind of strange."

"No stranger than all the other things going on around here," Mr. Turner said.

It was after school the next day. Mark was sitting in the Turner living room with Bill and his parents.

"But you think you figured out what's going on?" Mrs. Turner asked.

"Yes." Mark nodded. "First of all, the people you see aren't really in your house at all. Not as far as they're concerned anyway. They're in *their* house."

Mrs. Turner looked confused. "You mean, they lived in a house that was built right here?"

"Almost," Mark said. "It was an old farmhouse that was torn down. Then the developer brought in a bunch of fill dirt. It happens all the time. So when your house got built, it was in the same place but—"

"It started out higher," Bill guessed. He started feeling excited. He was beginning to understand. "It's like our house is taller or something."

"You're right, Bill," Mark went on. "Your house is also a little bigger than the old farmhouse. But the rooms are arranged in precisely the same way."

"Precisely," Bill said. "That's your word, Dad."

Mr. Turner put a hand on Bill's shoulder. "You're right about that."

"So if your new house and the old farmhouse look the same, but one is taller, what do you think that means?" Mark asked.

Bill thought it over. "It means the people *do* have legs. I just can't see them. Because of what you said. The people aren't in my house. They're walking in the exact same places they used to walk, but in the old farmhouse. Where all the floors were lower. That's why we can't see their legs."

"That's what I think too," Mark said. He looked at Bill Turner's parents. "At TAPS we call this a 'residual haunting.' You see the ghosts, but they don't see you. They're in their own world, repeating the same things over and over. Like a tape player playing itself over and over again. It's as though they're stuck in their very own time warp."

"So how do we unstick them?" Mr. Turner asked.

"That's a very good question," Mark replied. "There's no sure way. No one way, either. Sometimes confronting the ghosts, trying to get them to see you, works."

"I want them to go away," Bill said.

Mrs. Turner made a sound of distress.

"I know," Mark said. "I don't tell very many people this, but I understand how you feel, Bill. My brother and I grew up in a haunted house. I was afraid too. Lots of times. But I told myself I could be brave, and you know what happened?"

"What?" Bill asked.

"The more I told myself I could be brave, the braver I got. My guess is, you can do that too. You're brave in ways you don't even know yet, Bill."

"Thank you for coming," Mr. Turner said. He stood up. "You've given us a lot to think about."

"I hope I helped," Mark said. He stood too. He shook Mr. Turner and Mrs. Turner's hands. Then he shook Bill's hand and gave him a business card.

"If you need to reach me, just call."

"I'm brave," Bill whispered to himself.

It sounded pretty convincing that afternoon when the sun

was out. Now, in the middle of the night, when everything was dark? Maybe not so much.

Bill wasn't about to let his own fear stop him, though. Mark Hammond said *he* learned to be brave. Braver than he thought he could be. Bill was determined to learn to be brave too. Brave enough to put his new plan into effect.

Project Scare the Ghost.

I can do this. I'm going to do this, he thought.

Bill was done with waiting for the legless man to come up the stairs. Done with hoping that the man wouldn't come. Bill *wanted* the legless ghost to come tonight.

Because tonight, Bill was going to be brave. Braver than ever before in his life. He was going to help his family. He was going to help the man—help *all* the ghosts move on.

He stood at the top of the stairs. His eyes searched the darkness below. Any minute now, the man would appear in the downstairs hall.

There he is! Bill's heart began to pound. He could feel the cold start to creep upward. It circled his ankles like fog. Slowly, slowly, the legless man began to climb the stairs.

Bill stayed right where he was. The cold was up to his knees now. Rising higher and higher. Now the cold was at his waist. Then his chest. Bill's breath came in short, hard gasps.

The legless man was halfway up the stairs now.

Wait, Bill said to himself. *Wait for it.*

The man was almost to the top of the stairs.

Bill's whole body felt strange—like a cross between a rock and Jell-O. Hard and soft. He was scared. But he also felt brave. Was he going to stand and fight—or run for his life?

Now!

Bill was brave. No two ways about it. Because he *did* run.

Straight down the stairs toward the legless ghost.

Straight *through* him!

Everything seemed to move in slow motion. Bill's body went numb with the cold. His eyesight went out of focus. He felt his legs buckle. He reached for the handrail on the stairs. His fingers closed around it.

Then he was through, on the other side of the ghost. Gasping for breath, Bill swung around.

The legless man stopped. He stood motionless two steps above Bill.

Slowly...ever so slowly...he turned around.

His eyes met Bill's. *He sees me!* Bill thought. *My plan is working!*

The expression on the man's face was puzzled. Like he couldn't quite figure out where he was. In that instant, Bill felt something change. The numbness vanished. He could see clearly again. He wasn't afraid of the legless man anymore.

Bill opened his mouth to tell the man everything was going to be all right. But he didn't say anything after all.

Because in a split second—between one blink of Bill's eyes and the next—the legless man was gone.

"And he hasn't been back," Mark told the TAPS team a few weeks later. "None of the legless spirits have returned. Bill's plan did the trick."

"That was a risky move," Jason said.

Mark nodded. "It was. When I said he was braver than he thought he was, I never imagined he would tackle the ghost head-on."

"Well, all's well that ends well," Grant said. "Though something tells me that kid may have a future as a member of the TAPS team."

"Funny you should say that," Mark replied. He pushed Bill's letter across the meeting room table toward Grant. "He wants to know how old he has to be to apply. I think *you* get to answer that one!"

THE
HAUNTING
OF
FORT
MIFFLIN

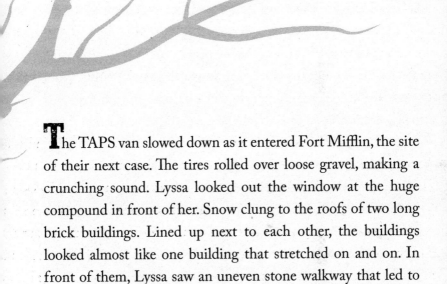

The TAPS van slowed down as it entered Fort Mifflin, the site of their next case. The tires rolled over loose gravel, making a crunching sound. Lyssa looked out the window at the huge compound in front of her. Snow clung to the roofs of two long brick buildings. Lined up next to each other, the buildings looked almost like one building that stretched on and on. In front of them, Lyssa saw an uneven stone walkway that led to another set of buildings. Past that were big fields, and even farther out was a high wall that went around the entire fort.

When Jason stopped the van, she and Mark piled out. Lyssa stretched her arms to the sky. Stretching felt good. The TAPS team drove almost five hours to get to the fort, which was just outside Philadelphia. Lyssa could see Grant and Jen and Mike approaching from the other van. The TAPS team was ready to investigate.

Mike and Mark had been talking about Fort Mifflin for months. The twins had all sorts of e-mails from people who went on tours of the fort. The visitors swore they had seen figures in windows, heard voices in the hallways, screams from other rooms. So when Jason and Grant got a call to come investigate, they organized the trip right away.

Now Lyssa could almost *feel* the history of the place. It floated all around her. But there was also something very gloomy about Fort Mifflin. The buildings seemed solid but worn down. Red brick showed underneath chipping paint. The peeling paint made them seem like spooky ruins.

A tall man appeared in the doorway of a building nearby and approached the group.

"Hi. You must be from TAPS. I'm Victor, the caretaker of Fort Mifflin."

Jason introduced the team, and everyone shook hands. Then Grant said, "Why don't we start with you telling us a little about the place?"

"Sure, I'd be happy to. My wife, Sarah, usually leads tours here. But she couldn't make it today. So I'll be your tour guide."

Lyssa and the others followed him toward the closest building.

"There's been a lot of history here. This fort was important in both the American Revolution and the Civil War. Before the Revolution, Benjamin Franklin headed a committee to make sure a fort was built that would protect Philadelphia. Fort Mifflin was built in 1771. Only six years later, the soldiers here held off the British Army so that General Washington could get his soldiers to Valley Forge."

"You mean George Washington, right?" Jen asked.

Victor nodded. "The fighting here lasted five weeks. It was the heaviest attack of the war. Hundreds of men were wounded. And 150 men lost their lives. They died right where you're standing."

Lyssa looked around her and shivered. She could almost see the heroic American soldiers being cut down by the British Army.

"Well, at least we won the war," Mike said with a grin.

"But not this battle," Victor told him. "The British ended up taking the fort. But if the soldiers here hadn't held them off so long, the Revolution might have ended very differently. They call this place 'The Fort That Saved America.' And that's only the beginning.

"After all that fighting, the fort was damaged so badly, it had to be built all over again."

Victor turned swiftly and marched forward, like a soldier himself. Lyssa moved quickly to keep pace with him. She breathed in the crisp winter air. There was an electric smell, like on days right before it starts to snow. But there wasn't a cloud in the sky.

Victor stopped in front of the archway of a building. The entrance of the arch was blocked with iron gates.

"The dungeon is through there," he said.

"The dungeon...that sounds so much worse than prison, but that's what it was, right?" Mark asked.

"That's right," Victor said. "It's always been called that, ever since it was built. The prisoners were kept in there. In the summer it was scorching hot. In the winter it was bitter cold. It wasn't a good place to be."

Lyssa looked in through the archway. The hall behind it was shadowy. She had to squint to see anything at all.

"What kind of paranormal activity has been reported in there?" she asked Victor.

"Well, it's hard to say. I don't like going in there at night. I get this real bad feeling, like somebody's watching me, like they don't want me in there."

"Who do you think could be watching you?"

"We have records of about thirty prisoners who died in there. Many froze to death, some starved. So I'm not sure exactly who it might be. But whoever it is definitely is not happy."

"Besides getting a weird feeling, have you ever *seen* anything strange in the dungeon?" Lyssa asked.

"I...There was one time. Out of the corner of my eye. I

thought I might have seen something, like a figure of a man huddled over. But by the time I turned to face it, it was gone."

Without another word Victor sprang ahead. As if he had to get away from the dungeon.

He led the team across a field to an old cannon next to a mound of dirt. In the middle of the mound was a crooked wooden door with a few rotting planks. Victor kneeled down in front of it. He put his fingers through a metal ring and pulled the door open. Tiny spiders scattered into the cracks of bricks as the door opened. A wobbly-looking wooden ladder plunged into the darkness below.

"This is Casemate 11. It's a new find. I discovered the door in the ground a few months ago. I was mowing the grass, and I saw it."

"What was this place used for?" Jason asked.

"A casemate is a room used to store guns and ammunition. Soldiers used them as places where they would fire on the enemy. But this one was used a little differently. When a prisoner got in trouble in the dungeon, they sent him down here. This was a solitary confinement area. It's quite a bit larger than just a single cell, though. There are a few different areas down there."

The TAPS group leaned over to get a look into the cavern. Loose dirt tumbled down the sides of the hole. Lyssa got a quick chill down her neck. She could imagine how awful it was to be a prisoner trapped inside. Like being buried alive.

"Actually, the casemate is one of the reasons I called you all in," Victor continued. "It's safe to go down there—the roof won't fall on your head or anything like that. But before we let tourists go in, we need to know if we're going to have other problems."

"What kind of other problems?" Lyssa asked.

"It's like a maze down there. Lots of twists and turns. You basically have to walk single file. If something was down there—something frightening—there'd be no getting away from it."

Victor leaned over and gently closed the wooden door.

"I've got one more place to show you, and then you're on your own."

He led them back across the field to a yellow building. It had a large balcony hanging over a porch. The team stood silently on the stone walkway in front of the porch steps.

"This was the officer's quarters," Victor said. "The fort's commander lived in there. But some people believe that someone else lives here now. The wife of Sergeant Pratt. It's a very sad story. Back in the 1800s, when the sergeant and his wife, Elizabeth, lived here, medicine wasn't what it is today. They had a little daughter who died, right up in that bedroom."

Victor raised his hand, pointing to a window next to the balcony.

"Elizabeth Pratt was so heartbroken that she cried for a week," he went on. "Everybody could hear her—from the prisoners in the dungeon to the soldiers in the mess hall. She wouldn't eat, wouldn't sleep. She just cried and cried for her poor daughter. After that, she couldn't take the pain anymore. She hanged herself right from that balcony."

"That's the saddest thing I ever heard!" Lyssa gasped.

"Some say that Elizabeth Pratt is still there. That her spirit has not left the room. Some tourists who passed by this building say they saw her in the window. Sometimes, near nightfall, they say they can hear her, weeping for her daughter."

In the Fort Mifflin dungeon, it got dark very quickly. Mike and Mark stood next to each other in the prison, underneath one of the few lightbulbs in the room. The bulbs threw a dim orangey light onto the floor. Mark leaned against the arched door frame. In front of him were rows of the original cots that the prisoners had slept on. Each cot had a thin green blanket on top.

"This is so cool!" Mark said, his voice echoing through the large room. "This place has so much history. If only these walls could talk."

"I'd like it better if the walls stayed quiet," Mike said. "This place is spooky enough already."

The air in the dungeon was still. The place was dead silent. A prickly feeling ran along Mark's spine. Mark shook it off. Then he let out a forced cough. He just needed to make a noise to break the quiet. Cold air stung his lungs as he breathed in.

"It's freezing tonight," he said. He looked down the long hall to the fireplace. "I wish there was a fire going in that thing right now."

Grant's voice came over the walkie-talkie. "Time to go dark." Mark was about to flick the switch off when his brother grabbed his arm.

"Wait a second," Mike said. He looked strangely at his brother, inspecting his face.

"What's wrong?" Mark asked.

"Are you shivering?"

"No. I brought gloves and a scarf. I'm fine."

Mike let go of Mark's arm.

"Do you hear that?" Mike whispered.

"Hear what?"

"That chattering sound. It sounds just like someone shivering. It's coming from somewhere in the middle of the room. Maybe it's just the windows rattling."

"Mike, there are no windows. This is a prison."

"What could make that sound, then? Don't you hear it?"

Mark felt a tingling in his hands. Yes, he could hear it now. It sounded just like teeth chattering. He glanced around, looking for a possible source of the sound. He found nothing that might make a rattle.

"I'm going to turn off the lights now," he said in a hushed tone. "Maybe the infrared camera will show us where the noise is coming from."

Mark turned off the switch. Inky darkness surrounded him. For a split second he couldn't see a thing. He reached out and touched his brother's arm.

"It stopped," Mike said. "The noise stopped."

Side by side, they made their way in between the rows of beds. A tiny beam of moonlight slipped in through the door behind them. This was the only light in the room. It cast a shadow in front of the brothers as they made their way down the hall.

In the dark, the details of the room were invisible. But when they looked on the IR camera's screen, they could see more. Everything in the room showed up as cool blue images. It was so cold in the room, Mark's hair felt stiff in his scalp. He looked at his brother. The blue light from the screen lit up Mike's face, making it look frozen in ice.

Suddenly Mike stopped. "Mark, look at this."

Mike pointed to the image on the screen of the bed in front of them. The bed was a deep navy blue, like the rest of the room.

Except for one spot. There was a small patch of green on the bed. The green area was on top of the blanket in the shape of an upside-down *V*, the wide part facing them.

"Mike, what's that green triangle on the screen? Why is that spot warmer than the rest of the bed?"

"I'm not sure."

Mark took a closer look.

"The green lines almost look like the imprint of legs. See? Like someone was sitting here and then got up," he said.

The shivering noise, Mark remembered just then. Mike said it came from the middle of the room—right where they were now standing.

"Yeah, I see that. If someone was sitting here, their thighs could have left some heat on the blanket," Mike said. "Who was in here tonight before us?"

"No one. It's just been us for the past hour. And it's so cold in here, even if someone was sitting on the bed before, all the heat would be gone by now."

"But if no one else was here…"

Mark's throat closed up as he swallowed. He stared at the screen. The camera was telling him there was someone sitting on the bed in front of him. But that was impossible. The only other person in the room was standing right next to him.

But when Mark looked up, there was no one on the bed. He walked over to touch the spot. He felt the smallest amount of warmth coming off the thin blanket.

"What can you see on the screen now?" he asked his brother.

"Your hand is red hot. The green part is still there too, below your hand."

Mark moved his fingers around. All he felt was the rough blanket. He took a step forward. The sound of his footstep bounced off the walls of the empty room.

"Is anybody here-*eer-eer-eer*?" his voice echoed. "Anyone?" His own words answered a moment later, saying back *"anyone, anyone, anyone…"*

Mark slowly turned his head from side to side, checking over the motionless room. Each bed looked exactly the same as the others.

"Mark!" Mike's voice was a harsh whisper.

On the camera screen a glowing yellow figure appeared at the end of the hall. It was the size and shape of a man. The glowing figure stood very still in front of the fireplace. It looked like a person trying to get warm.

Mark looked down the hall. He couldn't see the end of the room clearly. It was too dark. Everything blended together after a few feet. He got dizzy looking out into the darkness. "Hey!" he yelled. "You! By the fireplace!"

No answer.

"He's not moving," Mike whispered.

"Hello?"

After his echo died, there was silence again.

"It's still there, Mark...."

"Let's go—fast."

Gulping in chilly air, the twins ran to the other end of the dungeon. They stopped a few paces from the fireplace. Mike aimed the IR camera.

"There's nothing here!" he said. "The figure was right there a second ago!"

Grant opened the heavy door to the officer's quarters and walked inside. Jason was right behind him. They went over to the staircase, taking in the layout of the foyer. The first floor felt pretty normal. But that wasn't where Sergeant Pratt's wife had hanged herself.

At the bottom of the stairs they stopped.

"After you," Grant said.

Jason went ahead. Grant followed, carefully climbing the stairs. The wooden steps creaked under his feet.

"I can't stop thinking about Elizabeth Pratt," Jason said as he climbed the stairs. "That poor woman."

"I know," Grant said. "The story really stuck with me too. And based on what Victor said about hearing her at night, I think Elizabeth Pratt might be stuck *here*. She could be so attached to this place that her spirit just never left."

At the top of the stairs, Grant got the audio recorder ready. He took a moment and looked around. The glass used in the windows was old, like in a church. It wasn't completely flat, and it made the outside world look wavy and broken.

Grant stepped into the hall. His knees wobbled. Suddenly it felt as if the floor dropped beneath him, and he tumbled forward. He reached out for the wall to steady himself.

"Whoa! I almost fell over."

"Watch your step," Jason said. "Be careful—this floor isn't level. It's so old, it slants. It's like you're walking in a fun house."

Grant took a breath. The air was musty. It had that old-book smell. He took a cautious step forward and walked ahead of Jason to Elizabeth Pratt's bedroom.

He peered into the room from the doorway. There was a chair in the corner and a four-poster bed against the wall. The rest of the room was bare. The curtains to the balcony were open. He could see straight out through the windowed doors onto the balcony. There was something hypnotic about what he was looking at. He couldn't take his gaze away from the balcony.

Then he realized: he was looking at the last thing Elizabeth Pratt saw before she died.

Grant stepped into the room. He could sense Jason's presence behind him, but there was something else. Almost as if there were whispers too quiet for him to hear.

He turned on the audio recorder and spoke aloud. "Elizabeth?

My name is Grant. Don't be afraid of us. We just want to know more about you."

He took a step closer to the balcony.

"Are you here tonight, Elizabeth?"

Looking straight ahead, he could make out his own reflection in the balcony doors. It was distorted from the old glass. His face seemed pinched in and wavy. Slowly, he moved closer to the balcony.

"We know your daughter was very sick. You never had a chance to say good-bye." Grant was concentrating hard. All he saw was the window in front of him, his reflection shimmering in the glass. The rest of the room faded from his vision.

"Elizabeth, are you here? Maybe if you show yourself, you'll feel less alone...."

Grant's voice trailed off. His mind went blank. Staring past his reflection, he looked out into the night. He felt a terrible sadness. As if he had lost someone...

Then something grabbed his arm and yanked him backward. He snapped his head around, feeling pressure on his arm—and saw Jason gripping his sleeve. Jason's eyes were wide.

"What's wrong? Why'd you pull my sleeve?"

"Grant, did you hear that? Listen."

They both waited, completely silent.

Grant paid close attention to the sounds in the room. He could hear Jason's camera running and the grandfather clock ticking very softly downstairs. The hooting of an owl in a tree. Even the familiar sound of a mouse crawling in the wall.

Then he heard something else. At first he thought it was just a floorboard squeaking. Or an insect buzzing. The sound was high pitched and only lasted a second. Then it came back stronger. A shiver ran down his body. It was a voice, a child's voice.

"mommy! mommy!"

Grant's head whipped around.

"Hello? Is anybody there?"

No response.

"Elizabeth?"

After a few minutes of silence, Grant turned off the audio recorder. He looked at Jason.

"What was that?"

"It sounded like a little girl," Jason said. "It sounded like she was saying 'mommy.'"

Grant nodded. "That's exactly what I heard."

"Maybe it's not Elizabeth Pratt haunting this room," Jason said. "Maybe it's her daughter."

The group met up at the Central Command Center. Lyssa was sitting behind the monitors next to Jen. They'd been watching the camera footage and listening in on the audio all night.

"I know staying at Command Center is important," Lyssa said. "But it's nowhere near as exciting as gathering evidence."

Grant and Jason walked in just in time to hear Lyssa confess: "I never thought I'd be saying this. But I kind of miss being in the middle of things."

"There's still one more place we need to check out," Grant said. "You two up for it?"

Jen turned to Lyssa. She looked excited.

"You'd switch with us?" Lyssa asked Grant.

Grant smiled at her. "Casemate 11 is all yours. We've had enough action for one night."

The door to Casemate 11 was open wide. *Like a coffin,* Lyssa thought. Broken cobwebs lined the opening. Lyssa smelled the frozen grass, felt it crunch under her boots. She shone her flashlight down, lighting up the dirt floor ten feet below. She watched as Jen stepped onto the rickety ladder.

"Do you want me to go with you?" she asked Jen. "It's tight, but I think we can both fit. You don't have to go alone."

"No. The space is too small. I'll go first with the audio recorder. Then you go down with the video. If we go in together, we might mess up each other's evidence."

Jen started to make her way down the ladder. Lyssa watched her image get fainter and fainter until she was gone completely. In her mind she saw prisoners being forced down the hole. She could imagine their fear, knowing they might never come out.

"If you need anything, just yell. I'm not sure the walkie-talkies will work," Lyssa shouted down the hole.

"Okay," Jen shouted back.

Lyssa crouched by the door. Her mind went back to the prisoners. She could see the terror on their faces as the door clanged shut above them, blocking out all the light. How they lived stooped over, picking off the slimy bugs that crawled over their skin. They must have whispered to each other, planning ways to escape. But there was no way to escape. They were trapped in the dank blackness of the casemate.

Lyssa could hear Jen down below shuffling her feet. She could even make out a bit of Jen's voice talking into the recorder.

Then Jen's voice stopped. A few minutes went by.

"Jen, you all right?" Lyssa called down.

She aimed her flashlight down into Casemate 11. She could see Jen's footprints leading into the tunnel. None leading back.

"Jen?"

Then Lyssa heard a scream from deep down in the hole.

"Ahhhhhhhhh! LET GO OF ME!"

The scream echoed, and then Lyssa heard the sound of footsteps. Fast footsteps. She leaned over and saw the top of Jen's head as she struggled to climb the ladder and get out.

Finally, Lyssa reached down and grabbed Jen, and she scrambled out of the hole. Jen threw her arms around Lyssa and caught her breath.

"What happened?" Lyssa could feel Jen's chest heaving in and out.

"I was down there…It was so dark. I was asking questions. And then I felt something. A tickle on my neck. *Something* was tickling me. It raced all over my neck and onto my face. Then it started to scratch my face!"

"What was it?"

"I don't know, Lyssa. I don't want to know. It's so dark down there, even with the flashlight."

Suddenly Lyssa felt a small prickle on her face. It moved down to her chin, down to her throat. It felt like fingertips touching her. She jumped back. Frantically she grabbed at her neck.

Crunch.

She opened her hand. A crushed fat spider sat in the middle of her palm. "Yuck!"

Jen smiled and let out a sigh of relief. "That thing must've crawled off of me onto you," she said. "Didn't it feel exactly like a hand?"

Lyssa laughed. "Yeah, totally. I've never been this happy to see a dead bug in my life."

She wiped off the spider on the side of the door. She put new batteries in her flashlight and turned it on.

"I guess it's my turn," she said.

She put her foot on the ladder. The rung flexed beneath her weight. Step by step, she went lower and lower into the ground until she reached the floor.

She hopped off the ladder and hunched over. In one hand she held her flashlight. In the other she held the video recorder.

Slowly she made her way into the tunnel. Victor was right. It was like a maze. There were sharp turns every dozen feet that led to larger areas.

Lyssa didn't know what to look for. So she just kept walking straight ahead, very slowly, stopping at every curve, every cell. She didn't want to miss anything by going too quickly. After a few minutes in Casemate 11, her flashlight started to flicker.

That's strange, she thought. *I just put in brand-new batteries.*

She knocked its side, hoping the beam would return to full strength. She saw the floor in front of her dimming.

She called up to Jen, "My flashlight is acting funny."

But Jen didn't answer. Lyssa figured she must be pretty far into the tunnel if Jen couldn't hear her.

Then there was a sudden flash of light followed by complete

black. Lyssa shook the flashlight and flicked the switch a few times. But it was completely dead.

She flipped out the screen of the video camera and set it to night mode. She kept going forward, farther into Casemate 11. She came to a strange window cut out of stone with iron bars blocking it off. A metallic rusty smell filled her nose. Lyssa stopped to examine the cell.

She looked at the screen of the video camera. It was the only way she could see in the room. There wasn't much inside—a few rocks, little pieces of chain. She was getting ready to move on when she heard something behind her. Something that made her blood freeze.

It came from back near the ladder. A scraping noise. Like a person crawling on the ground.

"Jen?"

No one answered. But Lyssa could still hear the sound. She could feel a soft movement in the air. Her nose tickled. Something was moving around, kicking up dust.

"Jen, is that you?"

Lyssa turned, still looking at the camera screen. But she couldn't find what was making the noise. She moved toward it, placing each step slowly. The screen she was looking at was small. What if it wasn't picking something up? What if there was something it couldn't see hiding in the darkness?

"Anybody there?"

The scraping noise moved, coming toward her. Closer. It sounded like metal scratching against the brick walls.

There was a new noise now. A panting sound. Someone was definitely down there with her, crawling toward her. But no one was on the screen.

"Hello?"

Lyssa held her breath. Even though it was cold in the tunnel, she broke out into a sweat. She couldn't remember which way she came from. Which way was out.

Then the noises abruptly changed direction, as if they were going through the walls. Then it was quiet.

Lyssa set the camera down on the ground. The light from the video screen lit up the inside of the tunnel. It cast long shadows up against the ceiling. She turned her head to get a final look at the inside of the cell.

A shock jolted her against the wall. A flash of heat rushed to her ears as she let out a bloodcurdling scream.

Staring back at her was the scowling face of a man.

She saw him clearly. He had a big black mustache. His hands gripped the iron bars of the cell. Lyssa groped for the camcorder. But by the time she turned back around, the man was gone.

Lyssa rushed as fast as she could toward the ladder. The tunnel seemed to close in on her as she felt her way forward.

"You're almost there," she told herself. "You're almost there."

When she was finally aboveground again, she walked right past Jen. Jen said a few words to her, but Lyssa barely heard them. She barely saw the brick walls of the fort around her.

Though she knew she was aboveground, standing outside in the moonlight, all she could see was the face of the man with the mustache. Staring at her. As if he wanted to kill her.

Her walkie-talkie clicked and she heard Jason's voice. "Lyssa, Jen. Are you guys there?"

Lyssa shook herself out of her daze. She pressed the speak button on the walkie-talkie. "We're here," she said quietly.

"You don't sound so good," Grant said. "What went on down there?"

"I saw something. A man's face."

Bit by bit, she returned to reality. She looked over to Jen.

"Let's get back to Central Command," Jen said. "Then you can tell us what happened."

Jen shut the door to Casemate 11. Lyssa felt a little better, a little safer. She followed Jen across the field. All she wanted to do was get inside and warm up. But that face wouldn't leave her mind. It was there in front of her every time she closed her eyes.

It was vivid in her mind. Because it wasn't just a face. There was something in the man's eyes—something terrifying.

But it happened so quickly. And the face was gone so fast, only a split second after she'd first seen it. The farther Lyssa got from Casemate 11, the less sure she was of what she saw. Was it her imagination? Was it just strange shadows?

Or was it a ghost?

A week later, Lyssa and the rest of the TAPS team headed back to Fort Mifflin to share their evidence. Victor brought them into a room in the officer's quarters and sat everyone around a table.

"So, what's the final judgment?" he asked.

"This was a really interesting experience for us," Jason said. "The fort has so much cool history, and we all caught some evidence of paranormal activity."

Lyssa listened as Mark described his own experience. "In the dungeon, my brother and I heard a noise that sounded like a person shivering. It was very cold that night, you'll remember. We then caught an image of what looked like a man warming himself by the fireplace on the IR camera. But there was no one else in the room—and no fire in the fireplace."

Mike pointed out the image of the man on the screen to Victor.

"And when we were in Elizabeth Pratt's bedroom," Grant joined in, "both Jason and I heard this—"

He hit play on the audio recorder in front of him.

After a minute Victor rocked back in surprise. "It sounds like a little girl," the caretaker said. "It sounds like she's calling out '*Mommy!*'"

"That's what we thought too."

Grant looked at Lyssa, urging her to tell what she saw.

Lyssa cleared her throat. She was no longer totally sure she had seen that face. She knew very well that investigators had often been fooled. Sometimes they reported seeing faces, but the faces turned out to be just random patterns.

She started with the easy part. "In Casemate 11, I was able to capture sounds of someone crawling with my video camera. When I examined the video back at our headquarters, I was able to see strange moving shadows that matched the sounds.

"And there was something else," Lyssa went on. "I saw the face of a prisoner staring at me."

Victor sat up straight. "Do you have video of that too?"

"No, unfortunately I don't. I was too startled to get to the camera in time."

"By any chance, did the man have a mustache?" Victor asked.

Lyssa shuddered. "Yes, he did! How did you—"

"I didn't want to influence your investigation before it even started, so I didn't say anything. But Casemate 11 held a prisoner named William H. Howe. He was our most famous inmate.

He wrote to President Lincoln on several occasions asking for a pardon. A real nasty guy."

"What did he do?" Mark asked.

"He was found guilty of murder," Victor said.

Lyssa felt sick hearing that. No wonder the man looked as if he wanted to kill her. He was a murderer!

"William Howe was kept in Casemate 11 until he was executed," Victor explained. "We have a picture of him in the archives. He had a big mustache."

Lyssa nodded. "That sounds like the man I saw."

"That's really amazing," Jason said. "We think with all our evidence, and especially with the history of Casemate 11 and Lyssa's sighting, we can safely call Fort Mifflin haunted."

"But that doesn't mean you have to shut this place down," Grant added. "It's a great historical site. And the paranormal activity going on is what we call a residual haunting. These ghosts don't mean you any harm. In fact, they probably don't even know you're here. They are just so attached to this place, they can't leave. So they do the same things over and over."

"One thing, though," Lyssa said. "I'd have second thoughts about allowing visitors to go down into Casemate 11. I think William H. Howe might be better off left alone."

KNOCK KNOCK, WHO'S THERE?

"This is a really bad idea."

Ten-year-old Jasmine Anderson tugged on the front of her T-shirt, twisting the end of it around and around. She always did this when she was scared.

Lately, she was scared a *lot*.

"I don't want to go up to the attic," she said now. "That's where all the weird sounds started. Besides, we're not supposed to. Mom said so."

Her twelve-year-old sister, Tiffany, glared over her shoulder. The two were creeping up a steep and narrow set of stairs to the Anderson family attic. Tiffany first, then Jasmine. Usually, Jasmine hated it that Tiff always got to go first.

Not today, though.

"That was *before*," Tiff said. "What are you, still scared? The TAPS team came, you know. Even they couldn't find anything wrong."

That's true, Jasmine thought. *Sort of.*

The Ghost Hunters came last month. Mom called them because of the sounds: the bangs and the pounding. The thumps and the knocks. Sometimes the sounds were so quiet you could hardly hear them. Other times they were so loud you couldn't hear anything else.

Jasmine had a theory about them. One she hadn't shared with anyone else. She was sure there was a ghost.

Even so, nobody was more surprised than Jasmine when Mom actually called in TAPS for help. Mom said it was because she was at her wits' end. She was afraid to go to sleep at night. And it was getting so bad she thought she heard sounds even when there weren't any. Something had to be done.

The TAPS team came every week for a month. They put cameras and sound recorders all through the house. While Mom and Jasmine and Tiffany went to sleep, the team stayed up all night investigating the sounds. They came up with explanations for all of them. One by one.

One kind of banging was made by old water pipes in the basement. Another only happened when the heat went on. The one that scared Jasmine the most—the sound coming from the attic—was because of a loose shutter.

Mom made a "to-do" list. She got all the problems fixed. The sounds stopped. They hadn't been back. Not for two whole weeks now.

But Jasmine still wasn't convinced. She still thought there was a ghost somewhere in the house. Waiting for…she wasn't sure what. But Jasmine *was* sure she did *not* want to go up into the attic. The attic was where the whole thing started.

There was no way she was telling all that to Tiffany, though.

If Tiffany knew Jasmine was scared, it would only make her sister want to do it more. Tiff was always daring Jasmine to do stuff she didn't want to. And she never gave up. The fastest way to get Tiffany off her back about exploring the attic was to actually go there.

"Okay," Jasmine said. "You win. But just for a minute."

Tiffany smirked. "Right. Like you're in charge."

She turned around. The girls continued up. At the very top of the stairs was a door. Tiffany seized the big metal doorknob and turned it with a rattle.

Then she opened the door.

Squeeeaaak.

The door made a sound like fingernails on a blackboard as Tiffany pushed it open. Jasmine shivered. More than anything in the world she wanted to turn around and go back down those creepy, narrow stairs to the safety of her own bedroom.

If she did, Tiffany would never let her live it down.

121

She kept on going into the attic. It wasn't as bad as she thought. It was worse.

How long since anyone came up here? Jasmine wondered.

She didn't know. The attic was off-limits for as long as she could remember.

I can see why, Jasmine thought.

The attic was long and narrow. The steep slope of the roof made it hard to stand all the way up. The floor was covered with a thick layer of dust. Even the tiniest movement made Jasmine feel like she had to sneeze. She covered her nose.

The only light came from a window at the far end, opposite the door. It was hard to see, but Jasmine thought she could pick out strange shapes pushed back into the corners of the room. Like somebody was trying to hide them.

Hanging down from the ceiling was a single lightbulb.

"There's got to be a light switch," Tiffany whispered. "Find it."

"How come I have to be the one?" Jasmine hissed.

"Because," Tiffany said. "I said so. Besides, I want to explore."

"Tiff, wait!" Jasmine protested. But it was too late. Tiffany was already on her way across the attic, her footsteps stirring up the dust.

Jasmine reached out with her right hand and felt along the wall. A light switch was usually right by the door, wasn't it?

Jasmine's exploring fingers encountered something soft and sticky. She yanked her hand away with a sharp cry.

"Be quiet!" Tiffany hissed. She spun around. "Mom might hear you and then she—"

BANG! BANG!

BANG! BANG!

Tiffany gave a squeal and sprinted back toward the door. Jasmine met her halfway. The two girls clung together as the noise continued.

BANG. BANG BANG!

It was right above their heads. Like someone was throwing enormous rocks onto the roof hard enough to shake the house. Dust rained down onto the girls' heads.

"It's not supposed to happen anymore!" Jasmine wailed. "Mom did everything they said to. That was supposed to make it stop!"

As if it heard her, the noises came again, louder than ever.

BANG BANG BANG BANG!

"Girls!" They heard their mother's worried voice. "I can't find you! Where are you?"

"Mom!" Jasmine shouted. "Mom, we're up here! We're in the attic."

"Hold on," their mother shouted. "I'm coming!"

Jasmine could hear her mother's footsteps coming closer as she climbed up and up and up. *Run!* her mind said. But her legs refused to obey. They held her in place as if they were turned to stone.

She could hear the huff and puff of her mother's breathing

now. A second later she saw her mother's frightened face appear on the attic stairs. She was almost to the door.

"Mom," Jasmine sobbed out. "Mom!"

BANG BANG!

Jasmine let go of Tiffany and covered her ears. The pounding was so loud. Mom was at the door now. She was reaching out toward them.

BANG!

There was a last burst of sound. Then, before Jasmine's terrified eyes, the attic door slammed shut. She and Tiffany were trapped.

"Noooo!" Jasmine cried.

All of a sudden, her legs worked. She dashed to the door. She seized the doorknob with both hands and yanked with all her might.

The door flew open! Jasmine tumbled forward into her mother's arms.

"I know what it is, Mom. I know what's making the sounds," she sobbed out. "It's a ghost. It has to be. It has to be a ghost."

"TAPS team, we have a problem."

Everyone turned toward Jason in surprise.

"What kind of a problem, Jay?" Grant asked.

Jason sighed.

"That was Mrs. Anderson on the phone."

"Anderson…Anderson…" Mike said out loud as he tried to remember. He snapped his fingers. "I know. I've got it. The lady in Connecticut with the two daughters, right?"

"That's right," Jason said. "Good memory, Mike."

"Actually," Mike confessed. "It wasn't all that hard. That house really reminded me of the one where Mark and I grew up. I think it was even built at about the same time."

"1860," Mark agreed. "I remember from my research. Right before the start of the Civil War. It reminded me of our house too. Some rooms big and bright. Others tiny and dark. Sort of like whoever built it couldn't make up his mind."

"Why did Mrs. Anderson call, Jason?" Jen asked.

"Don't tell me the sounds are back," Mike said, before Jason could reply.

Jason nodded. "Yeah, they are. Why don't you tell Jen about the case, Mike? I think she was on vacation when we worked that one."

"Mrs. Anderson first called us almost two months ago," Mike explained. "She and her daughters were being frightened by odd sounds. Banging, knocking, and pounding all through the house. Sometimes it only lasted a couple of minutes. But other nights it went on for hours. There was no way to tell ahead of time.

"We pretty much did standard operating procedure. Cameras and sound recorders throughout the house. We spent about a month, all told. Though, of course, we weren't there every single night. The cameras never did pick up anything. But we came back with a *lot* of sound. I could even play some for you, if you like. I'm sure I've got the CDs around here someplace."

"That's a good idea," Jason said.

"Give me half a sec," Mike said.

"What kind of conclusions did you guys reach?" Jen asked as Mike flipped quickly through his CDs.

"We debunked every single sound," Jason replied. "It's an old house, like Mike said. I can't remember every detail. But it was things like loose shutters and pipes. We gave our findings to Mrs. Anderson. She made a to-do list and got some repairs done. After that the sounds stopped."

"Until now," Jen said.

"Yeah," Jason answered. "Until now."

"Got it!" Mike announced. "Let me just cue it up." He slid the CD into his laptop. "You know," he went on. "It's kind of interesting that Mrs. Anderson called. I always wondered if there was something we missed."

"What happened this time?" Lyssa wanted to know.

"The two girls went up into the attic," Jason said. "They heard this super-loud banging sound right above their heads. It shook the whole house. It was even strong enough to swing the door closed. For a couple of minutes the girls got trapped in the attic with their mom on the wrong side of the door."

"Wow," Jen commented. "Talk about a freak-out."

"You're right," Jason said. "It was. For everyone."

"Maybe it was some kind of animal," Lyssa suggested. "You know, like a raccoon. They're big and heavy."

"There's no way to know," Jason said. "That's just the problem."

"Okay," Mike said. "Here we go. Everybody ready?"

"Go ahead," Grant said.

"This is the upstairs attic shutter," Mike said.

Jen leaned forward as the sound came on.

Clack clack clack clack

Clack clack clack

Clack clack clack clack

Clack clack clack

There was a pause. Then the noise repeated. Jen thought it even had the same rhythm.

"Thanks, Mike," she said. "I think I've heard enough. It sounds like a shutter. But maybe I only think that because I knew what it was ahead of time."

Mike pressed a button and the sound fell silent.

"So," Jen asked. "What now?"

"Mrs. Anderson would like us to come back," Jason answered. "But I don't know. Our caseload is pretty heavy."

The month ahead was super-busy. Jason and Grant were going away for several weeks to investigate a site in California. That left just Jen, Lyssa, and the Hammond twins behind in Rhode Island.

"What did you tell her?" Lyssa asked.

"I suggested a 'wait and see' approach," Jason said. "If this turns out to be a onetime thing—"

"Then it probably *was* something like raccoons, like Lyssa suggested," Jen finished up.

"Right." Jason nodded.

"But if something else happens, you want us to go and check it out," Mike said.

"I do," Jason said. "I agree with you, Mike. I know we debunked every single sound, but I always had the sense there was something going on in the Anderson house. Something we couldn't quite put our fingers on."

"Sounds like the TAPS spider-sense at work," Mark teased.

"I'll go back over all the audio recordings. Just in case," Mike offered.

"Thanks," Jason said. "I was hoping you'd say that. Maybe *your* spider-sense can find something we missed the first time around."

"Come on, Jen. Just one more story!"

"I already read you three stories each!" Jen said with a laugh. "That's enough for tonight, you little monsters. Go brush your teeth and hop into bed. I'm going to check on the baby. Then I'll come tuck you in."

tood up and shooed the next-door neighbor kids off the

couch. Tony and Skye were seven and five. Jen babysat for them sometimes so their parents could go out.

Quietly, she tiptoed into the baby's room. Baby Julie was just six months old. She was sprawled on her back, sleeping with her mouth open. The sight made Jen smile.

She leaned over the crib. When she straightened up, she brushed against the mobile hanging above the crib. Moons and stars swayed and danced. Jen picked out the mobile herself. It was attached to a music box that played "Twinkle, Twinkle, Little Star."

All of a sudden, she felt a small hand in hers. Jen looked down. Tony and Skye smiled up at her. They came into the room so quietly Jen didn't even know they were there until Tony took her by the hand. Skye was standing at her older brother's side.

"Shhh." Jen put a finger to her lips.

Tony mimicked the action. Then he gave her hand a tug. Jen leaned down.

"Jen," he breathed into her ear. "I want to play the song about the star."

"Okay," Jen said. The sound was gentle and quiet. She didn't think it would wake up the baby. "I'll boost you up."

She lifted Tony in her arms so he could wind the music box. A moment later, the song began to play.

Twinkle, twinkle,
little star.

How I wonder
what you are.

Jen settled Tony onto her hip and hummed along. Her fingers tapped out the rhythm on the crib railing.

Tap tap tap tap
Tap tap tap
Tap tap tap tap
Tap tap TAP

All of a sudden, Jen stopped. Her fingers halted in midair. Her whole body seemed to tingle with electric shock.

Take it easy, Jen, she thought.

She did it again.

Twinkle, twinkle, *Tap tap tap tap*
little star. *Tap tap tap*
How I wonder *Tap tap tap tap*
what you are. *Tap tap tap*

That's it. That's really it, Jen thought. More than anything she wanted to run for the phone. But she didn't want to freak the kids.

"Okay, guys," she whispered. "Let's go out to the living room. I need to make a phone call."

"Wait a minute," Mike said a couple of minutes later. "Slow down, Jen. It's *what*?"

"'Twinkle, Twinkle, Little Star,'" Jen said into her cell. "That's what the sounds at the Anderson house are doing. They're playing 'Twinkle, Twinkle, Little Star.'"

"You have got to be kidding me," Mike said. "I've been listening to the audio for hours and I never picked up on that."

"Listen to them again," Jen said. "Now that you know. I'm babysitting so I can't get to the office right away. I'll come as soon as the kids' parents get home."

"I'll call Mark and Lyssa," Mike said. "Get them over here too. Jen, I've gotta ask this. How on earth did you figure it out?"

"I had help," Jen said, "from a seven-year-old."

"Okay, I just have to say this," Lyssa said. "Wow!"

It was a couple of hours later. The team, minus Jason and Grant, were in the TAPS office. Mike just finished playing back the audio.

There was no question about it. Every single knock, thump, and bang in the Anderson house was to the beat of "Twinkle, Twinkle, Little Star."

"Wow is right," Jen agreed. "So what do we do now?"

"I've been thinking about that," Mike said. "Did you ever see *Close Encounters of the Third Kind*?"

"Oh, no!" Jen groaned. "Please tell me this is from another ancient sci-fi movie."

"It's not ancient," Mike protested. "Just from 1977."

"Which would be before we were born."

"It's in color," Mark piped up. "Does that help?"

"Hey—wait a minute," Lyssa broke in. "I've seen that movie. It's great. I remember this guy builds a mountain out of his mashed potatoes."

"We're going to build a mountain out of mashed potatoes?" Jen exclaimed.

"Of course not," Mike said. "The part I'm talking about—"

"Although it *would* be really cool," Mark interrupted. "I've kind of always wanted to."

"Stop!" Mike cried. Silence. Mike waited until he was sure nobody else was going to interrupt.

"Forget the mashed potatoes," he went on. "There's this really cool part where humans and aliens make contact for the first time. The alien spaceship plays a series of musical notes. The humans play them back. Then the aliens respond. In other words, they *communicate*."

"Oh, I get it," Jen said, her tone excited. "You think maybe that's wh— going on at the Anderson house. Maybe there's an entity— —en, but a spirit. And it's trying to communicate."

"Yes!" Mike exclaimed. "And it's doing it by banging out 'Twinkle, Twinkle, Little Star.' So if we went to the house and played the song back..."

"We might get a response," Mark finished up.

"I found just the version of 'Twinkle, Twinkle' that I wanted while I was waiting for you guys to come in," Mike went on. "Jason and I both thought there was something else going on in the Anderson house. Something we couldn't put our fingers on. Maybe this is it. I think playing back the song is worth a try."

"I think so too," Jen said. She looked at Mark and Lyssa. "You guys?"

They nodded.

"Okay," Mike said. "In that case, I think we should call Jason and Grant in California and see what they say."

"Let's do it," Jen said.

Mike made the call.

"Okay," Mike said. "All set?"

"I'm as ready as I'll ever be," Jen said.

She and Mike were in the Andersons' living room. It was early evening. Mrs. Anderson was in her room. The girls were spending the night with friends. There were audio recorders in almost every room in the house.

Mike and Jen had his laptop. In it was the CD of "Twinkle, Twinkle, Little Star" that Mike made.

"Okay," Mike said. "Let *Operation Close Encounter* begin."

He pushed the play button on the laptop. The sound of a child's toy piano filled the room. Jen smiled in spite of herself. She had a piano just like that when she was little. She didn't think there was anything else on earth that made that kind of sound.

Plink plink plink plink
Plink plank plonk
Plink plink plink plink
Plink plank plonk

Mike and Jen let the song play all the way through. Then they played it a second time. Mike switched off the sound. He and Jen both stood still. Jen was listening so hard she realized she was holding her breath.

Nothing.

Jen let her breath out. "Try it again," she said.

Mike reached for the play button.

Before he could press it, one of the living room windows began to lift up, then slam back down.

Thump thump thump thump
Thump thump thump

" doing it," Jen whispered. "It's playing the song."

thump thump thump

134

Thump thump thump

There was a pause. The window stayed closed.

"Now what?" Jen whispered. "Do you think we should play the song again?"

"Maybe," Mike said. He reached toward the button.

BANG slam! BANG slam! BANG slam slam!

"What is that?" Lyssa cried out. "Where's it coming from?"

"This way," Mike said. "I think it's coming from the kitchen."

The two began to sprint in the direction of the sound. As they did, they heard the window in the living room start up again.

"You stay in the living room," Jen panted. "I'll go check out the kitchen."

She took two steps. Then she and Mike both heard something begin to pound on the floor right above their heads.

"It's upstairs now!" Jen cried. "It's all over the house."

"I know," Mike said. "I know. I'm going to turn the CD back on."

He sprinted for the laptop. He hit the button and turned up the volume. The sound of the toy piano poured out.

The whole house was shaking now, thumping and pounding to the beat of "Twinkle, Twinkle, Little Star." Jen and Mike stood in the living room gazing at each other with wide eyes. Neither of them had ever experienced anything like this.

Then, without warning, the sound over their heads stopped.

They could still hear the banging from the kitchen. Then that quieted down too. One by one, all the noises in the house came to an end. All the endless "Twinkle, Twinkle, Little Stars." Until only the toy piano recording was left playing the tune.

Mike leaned over to turn it off.

"No, don't," Jen suddenly said. "Let it play for a while. But turn it down."

Mike turned down the volume. The sound of the toy piano was sweet and peaceful now.

He and Jen stared at each other. They were breathing hard, as if they had just ran a race. All around them, the house was quiet as if it had never made a sound at all, as if it was settling down to sleep at last.

"I wonder if that's what the entity wanted all along," Jen said in a hushed whisper.

"What?" Mike asked.

"A lullaby."

"That was really creative thinking on the Anderson case," Jason said. "Good work, guys."

It was a couple of weeks later. Jason and Grant were back from California.

"Has there been any more activity since your visit?" Grant asked.

Mike shook his head. "None. I'm really happy about that. Don't get me wrong. I just wish I understood *why*."

"We may never know," Grant said. "We don't, a lot of times."

"Did your background research turn up anything?" Jason asked Mark.

"It didn't, really," Mark replied. "That house has been in Mrs. Anderson's family ever since it was built. Kind of like the house where Mike and I grew up. She has really good family records. People have died in the house over the years. You would expect that in a house that old.

"But no children. I didn't find anything that would explain why a lullaby might be so important."

"But we *do* know we made the Andersons feel better," Mike said. "That has to count for something."

"It certainly does," Jason said. He stood up from the conference table. "I say we all go home. Anybody got any special plans this weekend?"

"I'm making mashed potatoes," Mark said at once.

"Mashed potatoes?" Grant echoed.

"Don't ask!" Jen said with a laugh. "I'm not so sure you want to know!"

THE JEALOUS GHOST

*I*t came down the hall.

Tall. Dark. Terrifying.

Lips pulled back in a soundless snarl. Eyes that burned like coals. Arms reached out to grab and hold on tight. Fingers curved like claws, twitching as if they could already feel their victim's throat.

Step by step. The thing she was afraid to name came toward her. And she was trapped at the end of a dead-end hallway.

She felt the sob rise in her throat. She had time for one last breath. One last, desperate scream.

And then the thing was on her!

"Aaaaaaaaaaahh!" Jen Shorewood cried.

She jolted back in her chair, almost tipping it over. Then she started laughing. Lyssa and the Hammond twins joined in.

"I can't believe this dumb movie scared you," Mike said. He reached over and paused the movie playing on the laptop. The picture froze on the screen. The creature was in the shadows, and all you could see were his bloody claws.

"I know," Jen groaned. She shook her head. "Big Ghost Hunter, huh? I'm pathetic."

"Extremely," Mike said.

Jen reached out and socked him on the arm. "Thanks a lot!"

At that moment, the door to the TAPS office opened as Jason and Grant came in along with a blast of chilly air. It was October 30. The weather was clear and cold.

"Hey, guys," Jason said. He shrugged out of his coat. He and Grant were just back from giving a talk. "You're here late. What's going on?"

"We're having a Halloween film festival," Mike said. "I just freaked Jen out. She totally squealed like a girl."

"I *am* a girl," Jen said. "And I did not squeal. At least not very much."

"What did I miss?" Grant asked. Grant loved scary movies. Monsters. Sci-fi. And ghosts, of course. He particularly liked the older black-and-white horror movies. "What's this one about?"

"A ghost," Mike said. "What else?"

"Awesome," Grant replied. He came over to look at the laptop screen. "That's it right there?"

"Yep." Mark Hammond nodded. "You can't really see it there, though. If you want, we can go back…"

"In the meantime, let me guess," Grant said. "Chalky white skin and glowing red eyes."

"And claws," Jason put in. "Claws always come in handy. Don't forget those."

"You got it," Mike agreed with a laugh.

He punched a button and the picture on the screen began to move. The ghost began pulling itself up a wall.

Grant gave a sigh. "I have to say this. I know you guys have heard it before. Ghosts are just dead people. They're not monsters. They don't have super-strength."

"They don't go around killing people," Jason added.

"But sometimes they *do* act out against the living," Jen said.

"That's true. We've had some cases like that," Jason said. "Grant, remember the Maguires?"

"The Maguires." Grant frowned. Then his face cleared. "Okay, yeah. I remember. The Case of the Jealous Ghost. It was what—about three years ago?"

"I think that's about right," Jason said. "And it happened this month."

"Wait a minute," Jen said. "You're saying you investigated a case with movie-type scares? In October? Right before Halloween?"

"Yes," Grant said. "I guess so." He looked at the faces of the team. Four sets of curious eyes stared right back.

"I suppose you want me to tell you more…"

"We got the call about a week before Halloween," Grant began the story. "A woman named Karen Maguire. She said she wanted to talk to us about some incidents in her home.

"I remember the call very clearly. It was different from a lot of the calls we get. Usually when people call, they sound pretty upset. They've seen or heard things they can't explain. They're worried that their home doesn't feel safe to them anymore. They're on edge.

"Karen wasn't like that at all. She was calm. Very calm. Very clear."

Grant gazed from person to person. "But right from the beginning, I had the feeling there was something she didn't want to tell us."

"What *did* she say?" Jen asked.

"Karen told me that she and her husband, Tom, recently moved into a new house. Tom travels a lot for his job. Sometimes he's gone for a couple of weeks."

"The first time he went away," Jason picked up the tale, "Karen was left completely alone in the new house. But right away, Karen began to feel that she *wasn't* alone. She said she felt like somebody was watching her all the time. She would walk into a room, and she just had a sense that someone else was there."

"Karen never actually *saw* a spirit," Grant explained. "But she was absolutely convinced she was not alone."

"Was she freaked?" Jen asked. "Scared?"

"No. That was the strange part," Grant went on. "It was almost as if she thought of this spirit as a friend."

"He opened doors for her, turned the heat and the lights on right before she got home. Once, Karen left the iron on by mistake. When she hurried back to it, the iron had been unplugged. Karen believed the spirit unplugged it."

"You said *he*," Lyssa said. "I thought Karen never saw this spirit. How could she know the spirit was a man?"

"She said she just *felt* it," Jason explained. "She felt that she was important to the spirit. That's how we figured out what she didn't want to talk about. She actually felt weird about calling us. Like she was being unfair to the spirit—to *him*."

"So why did she call TAPS?" Mark asked.

"Things changed at the house. The spirit changed. Everything changed when her husband came home," Grant said.

"The spirit didn't treat Tom the way he treated Karen. He didn't open doors for Tom. He slammed them in Tom's face. He didn't turn on the lights and make Tom feel at home. He locked him out of the house sometimes. Tom no longer felt at all comfortable in his own home.

"Then it got really scary. The spirit began to appear in the bedroom every night. It stood near Tom's side of the bed. It leaned over him. Like some big, dark cloud. Tom didn't want to give in to his fear, but he couldn't sleep. He was really scared. He started sleeping in the guest room."

"I can't say I blame him!" Mike said. "That's pretty harsh. I mean, who wants to be afraid to sleep in their own bed at night?"

"Exactly," Grant said. "But it got even worse. The Maguires have a collection of African art. One day Tom was hanging an African mask on the wall. Tom was standing on a ladder. Suddenly he felt a hand grab his leg and pull. Hard. He lost his balance and fell.

"Karen found him on the floor, holding his ankle. The ankle was broken. That's when Karen decided enough was enough. In that moment when she saw Tom in pain, she realized she had a real problem.

"When she was alone, it was nice to feel the spirit wanted to protect her. But she didn't need to be protected from her own husband. That's when she realized she was dealing with a jealous ghost. And even worse was that Tom was in real danger. That's when she called us.

"I can still remember what it felt like to walk through the Maguires' front door that very first time," Grant continued. "The hairs on the back of my neck stood straight up. The energy of the whole house felt super-charged. I kept expecting to get a shock every time I touched something."

"We decided to start our investigation in the bedroom," Jason said. "Since that was where the spirit was actually showing itself. I remember Grant went downstairs to get some more audio recorders. I continued up to the bedroom. I was almost through the bedroom door when it slammed shut. Right in my face!"

Jason touched his nose. As if he could still feel the pain. "I got a bloody nose! I went down the hall to the bathroom to get cleaned up."

"Meanwhile, I came back upstairs and got to work setting up the camera," Grant went on. "I was up on a ladder when I felt a strong pull on my leg. I remembered what happened to Tom. So I held on tight to the sides of the ladder with all my strength."

"I was just coming out of the bathroom," Jason said. "I heard Grant yell. I ran in and found him clinging to the top of the ladder. The ladder was swaying from side to side. I grabbed it and held on tight until it was steady and Grant could climb down."

"And *then*, we went outside to talk. It seemed pretty clear to both of us what was going on—we were in a house with a jealous ghost. And now he thought *we* were the bad guys. He was coming after us," explained Grant.

"Wow!" said Jen. Her eyes were wide. "But you went back in, right?"

"Of course we did," Jason replied. "But we agreed to be extra careful. We agreed to stay in visual contact at *all* times."

"We went dark right after midnight," Grant went on. "The

Maguires were both in the downstairs guest room. Jay and I climbed the stairs.

"All that artwork looked a lot different at night. The masks looked like they were watching us. Walking up those stairs and down the hall to the bedroom felt as if it took hours."

"But finally we were standing outside the door to the Maguires' bedroom," Jason said. "The door was wide open. I put my arm against it to make sure it couldn't slam. Then Grant and I squeezed through the doorway together.

"And there *he* stood."

"There was a figure by Tom's side of the bed," Grant said. "Jay and I stopped cold. We've seen a lot of things, but this was like nothing we'd ever seen before.

"The figure rippled and shimmered. You know when you boil a pot of water? There's this point where the heat starts to rise. That's what the entity in the bedroom looked like. Only dark. We couldn't see through it.

"'Hello,' I finally said. 'I'm Grant and this is Jason. Karen asked us to come. We just want to know who you are. Can you find a way to tell us? Can you tell us what you want?'"

"What did it do?" Mike asked. "Did you get an answer?"

"No," Jason said. "Nothing we could see or hear. We tried again.

"I said to it, 'Karen wants you to know that we aren't here to hurt her. We want to help *you*.' But there was only silence. So we decided to go to the next step."

"Next step? What do you mean, next step?" Mark asked.

Grant took a deep breath. "We touched it."

"You *touched* it?" Lyssa exclaimed.

"We put our hands right through it." Jason nodded.

"It was definitely a strange feeling," Grant remembered. "Very cold. But also like static electricity. We felt as if we were touching the source of all the extra energy in the house."

"Touching it definitely got some sort of reaction," Jason said. "The figure flew up above our heads and darted out the door. Grant and I just stood there. Looking at each other and thinking, *Was that awesome or what?!*"

"And then," Grant said with a smile. "We both sat down."

"But what happened after that?" Jen asked. "You can't leave us hanging. It's just not right!"

"I don't know. It's getting kind of late," Grant said. He looked at his watch.

"Oh, Grant, *come on!*" the rest of the team cried.

Grant grinned. "All right. We spent a couple of months investigating the Maguire house. We never saw the figure again."

"But you must have come to some conclusions," Mark said. "What about the evidence? What did it show?"

"Not a lot, at first," Jason answered. "The cameras never did pick anything up. We had the audio running both day and night. Listening to it all took hours and hours."

"But finally," Grant said, "right about the time we thought our ears

149

would fall off, the audio gave us the clues that we were hoping for. We were able to make out *three names* that were repeated over and over.

"Klaus. Emily. John. We kept listening to those names over and over, trying to figure out what they meant. Who they were."

"Right. Who *were* they?" Mark asked. "And how were they connected to the Maguires' home?"

"Spoken like a true researcher," Grant said. "We did research on the house. We found out that John and Emily were a young couple. They moved into the house right after they got married. They were in love and happy to have their own home."

"But Emily had an old boyfriend, named Klaus," Jason continued. "He was really jealous. John and Emily went on their honeymoon. Then they returned to their new home. But Klaus was waiting for them. They all died."

"So Klaus is the spirit in the Maguire house?" Lyssa asked.

"We thought that at first," Jason said. "But then we changed our minds."

"How come?" Jen asked.

"Klaus claimed he loved Emily. But he killed her," Jason said. "He didn't protect her at all."

"But the spirit in the Maguire house did protect Karen," Grant continued. "He wanted to take care of her."

"It's almost like he wanted to make up for not protecting Emily from Klaus," Lyssa suggested. "So you think the spirit was John, not Klaus?"

"Yes." Jason nodded. "But the problem was that the spirit assumed that *any* guy who came into the house was there to cause harm. He couldn't see that Tom Maguire was actually the good guy."

"What did you finally do?" Mike asked.

"*We* didn't do anything," Grant replied. "It was Tom Maguire who figured out the solution. He had a man-to-man talk with John. He reminded him that Karen was *his* wife, not John's."

"But Tom didn't stop there," Jason said. "*He asked for John's help.* Tom asked John to keep an eye on Karen when he was gone. He said it would help him to know that Karen was safe. It would give him peace of mind when he was far away from home."

"And in exchange," Grant continued, "Tom asked John to give him and Karen some privacy when Tom was home."

"Did it work?" Jen asked.

"Well, we heard from the Maguires that the attacks on Tom stopped," Grant said.

"Wow," Mike said. "I don't think I've ever heard of anything like that before. The Maguires actually came up with a way to *keep* a spirit in their lives?"

"That's exactly what they did," Jason confirmed. "As far as we know, it's still working. We still get Christmas cards from them, don't we?"

"Do they sign them *Merry Christmas, from Tom, Karen, and John?*" Mark joked.

"Maybe they should," Grant said. "Maybe they should."

FRESH FROM THE GRAVE

Eli leaned against a gravestone. Its sharp edge dug into his back. Moss grew all over the sides. It felt cold and slimy against his skin. A chill raced down Eli's neck. He shook it off.

"You ready?" his friend Patrick asked.

"Definitely," Eli said. But he wasn't so sure.

"No wussing out now," warned Jake, his other friend.

"I'm not going to wuss out," Eli insisted. "I'm the one who thought of this, remember?"

Okay, maybe walking through the old graveyard wasn't the smartest idea. But it was a hot summer night, and there wasn't anything else to do. So why *not* go ghost hunting?

Jake flicked on his flashlight to make sure it worked. The

beam shone down on earthworms crawling over the dirt. They squirmed back underground when the light hit them. Jake turned the flashlight off.

Jake gave Eli his best evil grin. "Okay," he said. "Let's see how long you can stay in the graveyard with ghosts chasing you."

"No big deal," Eli said. Then he looked down. He saw a worm crawling over his shoe, leaving a trail of slime. He kicked it off.

"Fine," he said, and took a step forward.

The sun had set hours ago. The cemetery was all darkness and shadow. Eli had only been to the cemetery once before—but that had been during the day. At night it was totally different.

A pale crescent moon cast an eerie blue light over the graves. The tombstones were so old, they looked like crooked teeth pointing up out of the ground. They were definitely spooky, Eli decided. Really spooky because Eli knew that underneath them were dead people.

Row after row of dead people, shut up in coffins.

Rotting in the ground.

Eli didn't believe in ghosts. But what if—*somehow*—one of those dead people reached up and…

Snap!

Eli's foot crashed through something hard. His knees wobbled. His stomach dropped to his ankles.

"*Shhhh*," Patrick hissed. "You're not supposed to be stepping on the bones!"

Eli froze. His breath felt trapped in his chest. Did he really step on a dead person's bones?

He forced himself to look down. And saw a branch snapped in two. He began to breathe a little easier.

"Seriously, Eli," Patrick said. "You should show some respect."

Jake picked up the branch. "This used to *be* somebody," he said, dangling it in front of Eli's face.

"Ha, ha. Funny joke," said Eli.

They started walking again. It was growing even darker. Eli struggled to see what was in front of him.

"Jake, turn on the flashlight already. It's too dark."

"What? And let the ghosts know we're coming for them? I don't think so, Eli."

The boys moved deeper into the cemetery. Eli thought they might be getting a little lost. He didn't know his way around the graveyard that well. A terrible smell hit Eli's nose. A putrid odor forced its way up his nostrils. Eli coughed into his sleeve.

"Do you guys smell that? It's *horrible*. Something's rotting."

"Yeah, I smell it too," Jake said. "Like rotten eggs."

Patrick made a face. "No, it's worse. It's like when a mouse dies in your basement. And it stinks up the whole place. And it takes forever to find it and—"

"Okay, okay, we get it," Eli said. "Come on, keep moving. I don't want to be here all night."

They moved toward the oldest part of the cemetery. The ground felt like a damp sponge under his feet. He felt wet earth sucking at the soles of his running shoes. Every step seemed to pull him down into the wet soft ground. Pulling him into the cold darkness of the graves.

Eli's right hand scraped against a headstone. His knuckles burned. He stopped to rub his hand. It was bleeding. But that was good. That meant he was still alive. He wasn't sinking. He was just letting his imagination run away with him.

"What's going on?" Patrick asked. "Did you get a boo-boo?"

"Shut up," Eli said. He kept walking but more carefully, trying not to step on any of the graves... or touch any of the tombstones.

I'll be fine, he told himself. *As long as I don't touch any of the graves. No problem.*

Eli felt a flash of warm wind hit his face.

He looked over to the side and stopped. He was too startled to move any farther. His head felt light. He started to breathe faster.

In the distance, between two white headstones, Eli saw the figure of a tall man. The man moved back and forth. Like something trapped inside a cage. He paced and prowled between the two graves.

"Over there. Look!" Eli called in a low voice to his friends. Jake and Patrick swiveled around.

"Where?" Patrick asked.

"Shh, not so loud. About fifty feet to the left. That…shape…over there."

Jake and Patrick squinted where Eli pointed.

"There's nothing over there," Patrick said.

"Yeah, I don't see anything either," said Jake.

Eli couldn't believe his friends didn't see it! The figure was moving even faster now.

"No…look. There it is again."

"It's probably nothing. Just shadows."

The figure of the man stopped in its tracks. He looked straight at Eli. As if he was waiting for him.

"Are you blind?" Eli's voice was hoarse. A cold sweat trickled down his chest. "It's right there!"

"Then show us," Jake said. "I dare you."

Eli had never backed down from a dare in his life. He wasn't going to wimp out now.

He edged toward the figure of the tall man. But he bent low. He didn't want the man to see him. He didn't want the man to look at him ever again. He moved quietly, keeping clear of the gravestones. His heart raced so fast, he could feel it pumping in his ears.

Eli gasped. Suddenly the ground right in front of his feet lit up with a bright light.

Jake stood behind him. He had turned on the flashlight.

"I still don't see him," Jake said.

Eli straightened up. "Right in front of us," he said. But as Eli pointed, the shadowy figure vanished. Just as if it was never there.

They all walked over to the spot between the two gravestones. "This is where I saw him," Eli said.

"You're just seeing things," Jake said.

"Here, let me give you some glasses," Patrick said, making circles with his fingers and chasing after Eli.

"Hey, quit it!"

"Seriously. You think it was a guard or something?" Patrick asked.

"Maybe," Eli said. "I don't know. It was probably nothing."

Eli was lying. He knew someone had been there. Someone who stared right at him. But he didn't know how to make his friends believe that.

Eli glanced around. He heard a low sound like a raspy voice. It lasted only an instant and then it was gone.

"You guys say something?"

"I didn't say anything."

"Nope."

A few seconds later the sound came back. It grew louder. And louder.

"*Get out!*" it said.

Eli couldn't help it. He jumped back away from the raspy voice. One foot came down on soggy earth. His other foot went straight down into a hole.

He bit back a scream and grabbed onto the closest thing he could. A gravestone. A gravestone that felt ice cold even though it was the middle of summer.

Eli pulled his foot out of the hole. He let go of the tombstone.

"What's your problem?" Jake asked.

"Didn't you guys just hear that?" Eli said.

"Hear what?" Patrick asked.

"That voice. It was clear as day. I'm not kidding around."

"I didn't hear anything," Patrick said. "Come on, Eli. Quit trying to freak us out. The bugs are eating me alive. I'm sweaty. I'm hungry. Let's call it a night, okay?"

Eli was tired of feeling as if *he* was the one with a problem. He gave Patrick a friendly shove. "I think you're the one who's scared," he said.

"Yeah, right," Patrick said. "You're the one imagining ghosts. I'm not scared, because there's nothing out here to be scared of." He pushed Eli back harder.

Eli tripped over his feet and stumbled. He snagged his foot on something hard and fell to the ground. A dull thud sounded next to him.

Eli sat up. He felt sick to his stomach. Beads of sweat formed on his forehead. He saw a narrow trench in the ground beside him. He had toppled over a gravestone and it lay cracked in pieces that had scattered on the wet earth.

A mischievous smile came over Jake's face.

"Maybe we've been going about this the wrong way," he said. "Maybe these ghosts need to be woken up...."

"I wonder how long they've been waiting for us," Lyssa said. She was looking out the window as the TAPS van pulled up in front of the house. Mr. and Mrs. Burton stood next to the wooden gate. Their fifteen-year-old son, Eli, sat on the front steps. Even their dog, a big woolly mutt, was standing on the path that led to the house.

"Maybe they feel safer outside," said Grant. "From what Mrs. Burton said on the phone, all the weird stuff is going on *inside* the house."

"You didn't mention they had a dog," Lyssa said to Mike as they got out of the van.

"Scared?"

"No," she said firmly. "Allergic. Plus, it could be an important detail."

"Ah, don't worry, Lyssa. He's an outdoor dog."

"And how do you know that?"

"I got a strange vibration…" Mike said. "And the doghouse over there tipped me off."

Lyssa laughed. She never minded when the twins teased her.

Mrs. Burton greeted them and led them up the path to the house. Jason set down one of the heavy equipment bags. It hit the floor with a thump. Mrs. Burton started at the sound and Eli's eyes widened in alarm. Even Mr. Burton looked upset. Lyssa could see that they were all a little jumpy.

Inside, Lyssa and the Burton family sat down in the living room. The rest of the team split up to set up equipment and check out the house.

Lyssa looked around. The Burtons' living room was cozy. She could see the sunset through a picture window.

"You have a lovely home," she said. She pointed at a brightly painted clay candlestick on the end table. "That's so pretty."

"Eli made it for me," Mrs. Burton said. "At summer camp a few years ago. We never use candles, but I always keep it there so it's the first thing I see when I enter the house."

"Mom, please!" Eli looked as if he were about to die of embarrassment.

Lyssa took out her recorder. "There are a few questions I need to ask. The answers may help us in our investigation."

Mr. and Mrs. Burton nodded. They both looked worried. She

163

felt bad for them. Not too many people were like the twins, who had loved growing up in a haunted house.

Lyssa pressed the red record button and began the interview. "Okay, tell me what's been happening. When did it start?"

"About three weeks ago," Mrs. Burton said. "I was vacuuming Eli's room. I felt something pulling at me—like someone was grabbing my elbow—except no one was there."

"The next day we started hearing strange sounds in the night," Mr. Burton said. "I grew up in an old house. So I know all the creaks and rattles that houses can make. But this house was built four years ago. We're the only ones who've ever lived here. And we've never heard anything like those sounds before."

"What were these sounds like?" Lyssa asked.

Mr. Burton rubbed his jaw. "Like a wheezing. Almost like the voice of an old man. I kept thinking that if I listened hard enough, I could make out his words."

"And did you?"

Mr. Burton shook his head. "No. And this last week, I've heard those sounds every night."

Lyssa said, "Do you know where they're coming from?"

Mr. and Mrs. Burton looked at each other. Then Mr. Burton said, "The sounds seem to come from the direction of Eli's room. Our bedroom is just down the hall."

"Eli, do you ever hear the noise?" Lyssa asked.

"Yeah. I guess."

"Do you hear it in your room or outside it?"

Eli stared at the carpet and shrugged.

"Does it come from anywhere in particular? The closet? Under the floor? From above?"

"Just in the room."

Eli's answers were short, as if he wasn't very interested. *Maybe he's just shy,* she thought. *Or maybe he doesn't want anyone to know how scared he is.*

"It's more serious than noises," Mr. Burton said. "Sometimes an appliance will turn on right after I've switched it off. Or water will be running for no reason. Then when I check, the faucet will be shut off."

"And nothing like that has ever happened before? Have you had trouble with your wiring or your pipes?"

"Never," Mr. Burton said. "Also—" He hesitated. As if he was afraid she wouldn't believe him. "Things are being moved."

"You mean, you see things moving?"

"No. We find things in strange places. Places they shouldn't be. Every night, before I go to sleep, I put my wedding band next to the alarm clock. A few days ago, I woke up and it wasn't there. I searched for it everywhere. We found it on the carpet in front of Eli's room."

"That's not all," Mrs. Burton joined in. "Eli, remember your lunch money? On the counter?"

165

Lyssa looked at Eli. He ran a hand through his shaggy red hair. "It was nothing," he muttered.

"What happened, Eli?" Lyssa asked.

Eli shifted on the couch. He cracked his knuckles. "It really was no big deal."

"Eli, they need to know," his mother said.

"Fine. I put my lunch money out on the kitchen counter. The next day it was missing."

"Not just once, Eli," Mrs. Burton interrupted.

"A few times, okay," Eli said, sounding a little annoyed.

"Tell me how it happens," Lyssa said.

"I take my money and put it on the counter, next to my key. In the morning the key is there. The money's gone. That's all I know."

"That *is* pretty odd. When did this start?"

Eli focused back down at his feet. "I don't remember."

Lyssa could see Eli was growing more and more uncomfortable. "When was the last time this happened?"

"Two days ago."

"Has anything else of yours gone missing?"

"My pen. It's a fountain pen. A gift from my grandparents. I never use it. So I just keep it on my desk in its box. But last week it just kinda disappeared."

Lyssa turned to Eli's parents. "Could these strange incidents be connected to any other event? Maybe a death in the family? Or the anniversary of a death?"

Mr. Burton frowned. "Nothing I can think of."

"Me neither," said his wife.

Eli tapped his foot on the rug, making a soft, impatient sound.

"Eli, can you remember anything else?"

"No," he said. He looked past her shoulder. As if he found the wall very interesting.

"I know this must be tough for you," Lyssa said to Eli. "A lot of this activity seems to revolve around you. Is there any reason you can think of that a spirit might show up in your room? Is there an object in your room that might belong to someone who has died? Is there any reason a spirit might be attracted to the room—or to you?"

Eli stopped tapping his foot. For the first time he looked at her. "I—"

Lyssa heard a noise behind her. She turned around and saw the twins in the doorway.

"We're setting up the equipment now," Mike said. "Come on, Lyssa. We need your help in the kitchen."

"I'll be there in a minute," Lyssa told them. She turned back to Eli. "What were you going to say?"

Eli looked at his watch. "Just that I told my friend I'd call him." He fished a cell phone out of his pocket and walked out of the room.

Lyssa met up with the twins in the hall that led to Eli's room. It was late afternoon and the TAPS team was finishing the sweep of the house. Mark was holding the EMF detector.

"Let's check out the energy here," Mark said. "Lyssa, why don't you try it out?"

"Sure."

Lyssa held the black box in her hand. Taking small steps, she made her way down the hall. As she walked, she called out the readings on the meter. "I've got 2.2, now 3.4. Totally normal," Lyssa said.

Then she got closer to Eli's room. "I've got 5.7…wait… Whoa! It just jumped to 12.8!"

The twins ran over to check the meter themselves.

"That's a big jump," Mark said.

"There's nothing here. No microwave or cable box that could be giving off energy," Mike added.

Lyssa walked in the opposite direction, away from Eli's room. She stared at the EMF detector again. The level suddenly shot down from twelve to two.

"This is weird," she said. "The energy field shouldn't be changing this quickly."

Right then, Lyssa caught a noise coming from a different part of the house. It sounded like static from a radio. She followed the noise out to the hallway. She moved slowly. She placed each footstep carefully.

The sound became clearer. She could tell now it was running water. Mike and Mark stayed close behind Lyssa. She walked steadily to the hall bathroom.

The door was closed. There was no light coming from underneath. She was about to knock but hesitated. "Someone in there?" she called.

No answer.

She knocked. "Hello?"

She turned the knob. She pushed the door open a crack. She peeked in. The room was completely dark. She pushed the door fully open and turned on the lights.

Hot water streamed from the faucet. Steam billowed up like a cloud and fogged the mirror above the sink. Water poured out of the faucet so fast and hard that it splattered all over the counter.

"Someone left the faucet running?" Mark guessed.

"No." Lyssa's voice caught in her throat. "Mr. Burton said he turned everything off."

"Holy cow!" Mark exclaimed.

Lyssa never had to finish her sentence. Because just then—without anyone touching the faucet—the flow of water got thinner. Until it was barely a trickle.

As if someone was turning the knob.

Single drops of water plinked against the bottom of the sink. The mirror cleared. Droplets of water rolled off its silvery surface.

"Get Jason and Grant here right away," Lyssa said. "They should see this, now!"

At midnight the TAPS team completed their daytime sweep. Jason and Grant had examined the bathroom and found nothing wrong with the pipes or the faucets. Lyssa and Jen were in Eli's room, getting a good look at the place before they went dark. The room looked like an average boy's room: unmade bed. Desk with computer. Sports posters on the wall. Beanbag chair. Bookshelves jammed with comics, DVDs, and even a basketball.

But something was bothering Lyssa. It wasn't anything she could see. It was something she could feel. It was as if the air were made of prickly things. She didn't say anything to Jen. She just continued to wait in silence for the words that would change everything. Finally they heard the scratchy sound of the walkie-talkies.

Then Jason's voice. "Okay, everyone, let's go dark."

Jen, who was standing next to Eli's desk, turned off the desk lamp. Lyssa walked toward the wall switch. She stopped for a moment, closed her eyes, and then switched the light off. *Maybe in the dark that weird feeling will go away.* But the dark only made the feeling worse.

"Jen," she said. "Are you getting a strange vibe?"

"Yeah, I am. It's hard to describe. It's like the feeling you get that someone is behind you even though you don't see or hear anything."

"That's it exactly," Lyssa said as she turned on her recorder. "Okay, let's see if we can find out who's here with us.

"My name is Lyssa Frye," she began. "I'm here with Jennifer Shorewood. We mean you no harm. We only want to communicate with you. If there is a spirit present, please make yourself known."

She waited ten seconds. Silence.

"Can you tell us your name?"

No reply.

"Can you give us a sign? Is there something you want?"

"Help us out," Jen added. "Maybe we can help you."

Each time Lyssa waited ten seconds. She wanted to give the spirit time to respond.

Then she heard it. At first it was so faint, she thought she was imagining it. It sounded again, closer this time. It was a sad, muffled cry.

Lyssa's mouth went dry. She could hardly breathe.

"Jen," she whispered, "are you hearing that?"

"Oh, yeah."

Lyssa walked toward the sound. It seemed as if it was coming from Eli's bed. No, a little beyond. But there was nothing that could have made that moan. No air vent, no pipes.

Lyssa looked for the source of the sound. Then she froze. She grabbed on to Eli's night table, too excited and scared to move.

The chilling moan was back. It floated through the air. Louder and louder. Lyssa held her breath as the wail filled the room. Then the cry stopped. Lyssa felt her heart slow to normal. She let go of the table.

But the cry returned again. This time Lyssa peered out the window.

"Jen, you've got to see this."

Jen shot up out of the chair and grabbed Lyssa's shoulder. They looked down at the front yard.

Charley, the Burtons' dog, was sitting in the middle of the lawn…howling at the moon.

Jen let out a big sigh. Lyssa laughed. Jen laughed too but she added: "Just don't forget to tag the sound."

"Right. 12:18 AM, wailing sound: dog howling at the moon," Lyssa said clearly into the recorder. Then she turned to Jen and said, "Okay, let's go back to where we left off."

Lyssa walked around the edges of the room. She spoke to the spirit again. "Has someone in this house done something to make you unhappy? What are you trying to tell us? Why did you take Eli's money?"

Again, there was no answer to any of her questions. She wasn't sure what else to ask. Then, out of the corner of her eye, Lyssa noticed a small movement. She stopped cold. An electric shiver ran all over her body. Slowly she turned her head.

At first there was nothing. Just the door leading to the hall-way. And Jen, sitting in the desk chair, facing Lyssa.

Lyssa kept her eyes on the door. It was moving.

Inch by inch, it was shutting.

"Jen, turn around…"

Jen spun around. "The door," she whispered.

Slam! The door closed like someone on the other side yanked it shut.

"Jen, what *was* that?"

But Jen wasn't paying attention to Lyssa. She was already aiming the video camera at the door.

"I don't know what that was," Jen said. "It couldn't have been the wind, because the windows are closed."

Lyssa switched on her flashlight and examined the door

hinges. They weren't loose or broken. She looked around the door frame for something that might have caused the door to close. Maybe an air-conditioning duct? Or a spring connected to the door? No. She didn't find anything like that.

"This feels awful," Lyssa told Jen. "Like there's something here. And no matter what we do or say, it won't leave."

"Let's just double-check," Jen said.

She opened the door as wide as it was before and waited to see if it would slam shut on its own. Jen got down on the floor and put her flashlight on as well. "There's no way that door could have shut on its own," she said. "The bottom of the door presses into the carpet. The carpet keeps it in place. It would be impossible for the door to just close on its own."

Jen closed the door. Lyssa could see it took some effort.

Lyssa shuddered. If the door couldn't move on its own, then someone or some*thing* must have pushed it.

Jen flicked off her flashlight. She and Lyssa got up. Jen went back to the desk. She adjusted the setting on the IR camera.

Lyssa tried to piece together what was happening. Maybe the spirit wasn't speaking. But she felt as if something was letting them know it was there. She had seen its energy spike in the hall. It turned a faucet on—and off. And now it had slammed Eli's door.

Lyssa's throat went dry. She wasn't looking at any meter. But she could feel something on the other side of Eli's door. She was sure of it.

This time she didn't ask if Jen felt it too. She just gathered all her courage—and yanked open the door.

Eli stood in front of her in the hallway.

"Did you guys find anything?" he asked.

Lyssa and Jen looked at each other.

"Eli, does your door ever close on its own?" Lyssa asked.

"Why?"

"We just saw it slam itself shut. Does that usually happen?"

"Well…not exactly. I mean, I…I've never seen that happen before."

"You don't sound so sure."

"No, I'm sure. I've never seen it happen."

Lyssa's walkie-talkie crackled. She heard Grant's voice coming through.

"Let's pack it in, everybody. I think we've got all we can for tonight."

The crew met back at Central Command. They began packing up the equipment.

"This is the part that drives me crazy," Lyssa said to Jen as they walked out to the vans.

"You mean, leaving the site?" Jen asked.

"No, I mean having to wait until we can see what the instruments recorded."

Jen shrugged. "Well, you know how it goes. If we can't find proof of paranormal activity—"

"I know," Lyssa said. "I would never want to tell the Burtons that their house was haunted if there was really nothing there. But Jen, there *was* a spirit in that house with us. I could feel it."

As soon as the TAPS team drove off, Eli went back to his room. It was late. He slipped under the covers. It was a hot summer night, but the sheets felt cold and clammy.

Eli closed his eyes. He took deep breaths. He even counted sheep. But nothing worked. He couldn't sleep. Every time he closed his eyes, he saw the same image. The one from that night of the broken gravestone. The pieces shattered and thrown on the ground.

Then his mind went to the figure he had seen in the graveyard. The man pacing back and forth in the darkness. Then Eli thought about the sound he'd heard.

Get out! That's what the voice said. If only he had listened. If only he had run. If only he had stopped his friends. If only...

Then he would be able to sleep. Then he wouldn't be so afraid.

Then he wouldn't have a ghost after him!

I have to do something! Eli thought. Staying here tossing and turning was the worst. Eli slipped on his running shoes and tiptoed to his door. He felt like a blind man groping his way through the dark house, reaching for the walls to guide him. He held his breath and made his way down the hall. Every nerve in his body felt stretched tight. His brain screamed a warning. *Don't go! Don't go!*

But Eli knew he had to.

He snuck into the kitchen to get a flashlight from the drawer. Then he headed for the front door and reached for his jacket hanging on a hook.

As he pulled the jacket on, Eli saw something wedged in the umbrella stand. He stuck out his hand and grabbed it and gently tugged it loose.

He was holding the clay candlestick. The clay candlestick he made in summer camp, the one that no one ever used, the one that *always* stayed on the end table in the living room.

But not anymore. Now it was the candlestick the ghost had moved.

He put the candlestick down and fumbled with the door. His hand trembled as he turned the knob. Finally the front door swung open. Eli bolted down the moonlit street, chasing his own faint shadow toward the graveyard.

Eli caught his breath. He was standing in front of a high stone wall at the entrance to the cemetery. His lungs burned from running. The sun was not quite up and the sky was charcoal gray. A morning mist clung to the ground. It was so thick, Eli could hardly see what was in front of him.

He paused and smelled the damp air. Eli knew he had to take a step forward. He had to go into the graveyard. But his legs wouldn't move. They were locked in place like concrete. Last time, Patrick and Jake had been here. It was easier to pretend he was brave when he was with them. Now he was alone.

Was he really alone? Eli felt eyes staring at his back. He had the feeling he was being watched.

He spun around. But there was no one there in the thick, gray mist.

Eli's mind raced. A terrible thought was wedged in his mind. He could feel the truth of it in every cell of his body.

The ghost had followed him. Eli knew exactly how it had happened. The ghost had watched him toss and turn in bed. It followed him out of his room and trailed him all the way to the cemetery.

A crisp chill tingled against his cheek. Eli lifted his arm and turned on the flashlight. The mist reflected the beam back into his eyes, blinding him for a second. He quickly switched off the light.

Eli rubbed his face. He couldn't turn back now. He tried to turn off his brain and started walking into the graveyard. He wasn't even sure why he was doing this. Only that it was necessary.

Nothing in the cemetery looked familiar. In the charcoal light all the graves blended together. The white outlines of the tombstones were barely visible through the fog.

The feeling of being watched grew more intense. He couldn't shake it. The horrible stink of decay rose from the ground. Eli kept moving, stumbling through the fog. He heard a shushing sound and froze for a moment. Then looked up. It was only the leaves overhead.

Then he felt it again. Someone's gaze focused on the back of his head. He whirled around. All he could see behind him was fog. Eli looked around quickly. But there was no one in sight.

Eli started breathing faster. His chest heaved in and out. His hands rolled into fists. He was ready to run at the slightest sound.

"Who's there?" he yelled. "I know you're there."

He waited for an answer. Nothing.

He took a few steps forward. "Is anybody there?"

Eli felt a tickle on his leg. He took a few more steps. The tickle turned into a scratch. Then it started to hurt.

He felt a cold bony hand tighten around his ankle. He shook his leg, but the cold hand gripped tighter.

Eli took off. The faster he ran, the harder the hand clawed into his skin. It wouldn't let go. He fell to his side and thrashed his leg to break free.

He saw a fist-sized rock nearby. He grabbed it and raised it high, ready to smash the bony hand. Then Eli gasped. A dried-out wreath of dead flowers circled his ankle. Thorns, twigs, and wires wrapped around his ankle and dug into his skin. Eli pulled it off and shook his head in relief.

It was almost dawn. Eli could see the cemetery more clearly. He stood up and went to where he saw a gap in the row of gravestones. This was the spot. The headstone he'd knocked over lay at his feet in pieces. A few other gravestones lay knocked over and broken. The stone fragments were scattered like bread crumbs.

This was where Jake and Patrick tried to wake up the ghosts. They had been joking around. None of them thought it could really happen.

Eli crouched. He wasn't sure what he was looking for—maybe the name on the grave. The fog swirled around him, clouding his vision. Then he heard it. That voice. That raspy voice.

Get out! Just a whisper.

Get out! Deeper, more like a growl.

GET OUT! This time it was a shriek. And it was coming right at him!

Eli ran. Faster than he had ever run in his life. He didn't stop running until he was inside his front door. But even then he didn't feel safe. Whatever it was that was after him—it knew where he lived.

A few days after the Burton investigation, the team met at TAPS headquarters to discuss the evidence.

"So what have we got here?" Grant asked. He took a quick sip of hot coffee. "The Burtons could use some answers."

"After what I saw, I'd like some answers too," Lyssa said.

"Check this out," Jen called to the group.

She showed them an image on a computer screen. "This was taken by the thermal camera in Eli's room. I got it just after we saw the door close. Watch carefully. Did you see that bright orange spot?" She ran the picture back so they could all see the spot. It was right in the center of the door frame.

"The rest of the room is totally cool and showing all different shades of blue. But in that little area, it's hot. Very hot."

Jason and Grant came by to take a look. "Definitely a hot spot," Jason agreed.

"Could be evidence of a spirit," Grant added. "And the door and the faucet could also be evidence of the paranormal. But…"

"We're missing something," Lyssa said. "So many of the strange events seemed connected to Eli. The sounds. The missing money. The way his father's wedding band appeared in front of Eli's room. But Eli was so quiet, almost as if he wasn't interested. I think there's a piece of the puzzle that we don't have. And I have a feeling that the missing piece is with Eli. I think he's hiding it."

Lyssa was really pleased that she convinced Jason and Grant to let her talk to Eli one more time. They went to the Burton house without any of their equipment. This visit would be interview only.

They sat in the living room with Mr. and Mrs. Burton and their son. Eli was staring at the screen of his cell phone.

"I'm glad you're back," Mrs. Burton said to the TAPS team. She gave a shudder. "Is there a spirit in the house? Can you make it go away?"

"What did you find out?" Mr. Burton asked.

"We have some evidence pointing to the paranormal, but we don't have enough to be sure."

"Oh," Mr. Burton said. He looked disappointed. "Do you need to do more investigation?"

Lyssa spoke up. "We'd like to interview Eli again. Alone, if that's okay with you."

Mr. and Mrs. Burton looked at each other, a little confused. Eli seemed to be busy texting someone.

"Eli? But he already told you everything he knows," Mr. Burton said.

"We just have a few more questions," Lyssa said. "Things we've been wondering about since we saw the evidence."

Mrs. Burton nodded. "I guess that's fine. If you think it would help." She frowned at her son. "Eli, put that phone away."

Eli's parents got up to leave. "We'll be upstairs," Mr. Burton said.

Jason leaned forward a little. "Eli, we know there are things you didn't tell us. What's up?"

Eli's eyes moved from Lyssa to Jason to Grant.

"I told you guys everything I know," he finally said.

"No, you didn't," Lyssa said. "We know there's more to it."

This seemed to catch Eli's attention. He looked at Lyssa, a question in his eyes. Then he shook his head. "I can't," he said flatly. "If I tell you, you'll just tell my parents."

"We're not here to get you in trouble," Lyssa said. "We're here to help."

"I don't need your help."

"Oh? You're going to handle this on your own?" Jason said. "How's that been working for you so far?"

Eli sighed. "Not so great," he admitted.

"Please, Eli," Lyssa said. "Tell us what's really going on."

"Things got out of hand," Eli said quietly. "We didn't mean for anything to happen. But…" His voice dropped so low that Lyssa could barely hear him. "We did something terrible. And now I'm really scared."

"Who is 'we'?" Lyssa asked.

"Me and my friends. We went out to the graveyard one night. We were just bored. But I thought I saw something, and then I thought I heard something. And then one of my friends shoved me, and I knocked over a headstone. It was an accident, I swear."

"Is that *all* that happened?" Grant asked.

Eli shook his head. "Then my friends…They sort of went crazy. They knocked over a few more headstones. And all the weird stuff that's been happening in this house—it started right after that night."

Lyssa looked at Jason and Grant. They nodded to her in approval. Her instincts had proved right.

"Please don't tell my parents," Eli said. "They would be so upset with me. And those graves are so old. They were practically falling over by themselves."

"Like we said, it's not our business to get you in trouble," Grant told Eli. "But personally, I think *you* should tell your parents. They've had to deal with all this too. If you explain it to them the way you explained it to us, I'm sure they'll understand."

Eli nodded.

"And you have to make up for this somehow," Jason said. "It seems like you've offended a spirit. It's time to make up for that. Maybe you should go back to the graveyard to pay your respects. Cleaning up the area and apologizing seems like the right thing to do."

"Okay," Eli agreed. "I want this to stop. I'll do all of that." He gave them a quick grin. "In the daytime."

The only sound in TAPS headquarters was Lyssa clicking her pen against the desk.

"What a slow day," she said to Mark.

"Yeah, where did all the ghosts go?" he asked.

"Guess we're in a ghost-free zone right now," Mike spoke up.

Lyssa suddenly had an idea. "You know what?" she said. "I'm going to check in on the Burtons."

Lyssa picked up the phone and dialed the number. Eli's voice answered on the other end.

"Hi, Eli. It's Lyssa, from TAPS. I just called to see how you're doing."

"Hey, Lyssa," he said. "Things are good. I did exactly like you said. I went to the graveyard and apologized. Then I cleaned up everything."

"And…?"

"And our house has been normal ever since!" Eli said. Then he lowered his voice. "I don't know what would've happened if you guys didn't show up. Thanks so much for helping me."

"You're welcome," Lyssa said. It felt really great being able to help the Burtons.

Lyssa smiled and thought: sometimes being ghost free was a very good thing—even for a Ghost Hunter.

THE
GHOST
OF
GRANDMA
HELEN

" **W**here are you?" Miranda cried.

Four-year-old Miranda Johnston sat straight up in bed. Her back was pressed against the headboard. A strange tingling filled her whole body.

It didn't hurt. Not quite. But pretty close.

Miranda's pale blond hair tumbled around her shoulders as her head twisted from side to side. Her deep blue eyes were searching, peering into every corner of her bedroom.

"Where are you?" she asked again, in a whisper this time.

She hugged Polar Bear, her favorite stuffed animal, to her chest.

"I can't see you," Miranda whispered. "But I'm trying so hard!"

There was someone in the room with her. Miranda was only four years old, but she was absolutely sure about this.

"Don't be a…" She began to sing in a high, breathy voice. She rocked from side to side. *"Don't be a Little Louie Worrywart."*

Miranda giggled. Then she clapped a hand over her mouth to muffle the sound. The girl didn't want her parents to come in and make her go to sleep. Not now.

"Oh, Grandma! That's so funny. Okay. I promise not to tell."

"Miranda…sweetheart. Who are you talking to?"

Miranda's head jerked around. Her mother stood in the shadows of the bedroom doorway.

"What's the matter, Mommy?" she asked. "You look funny." Her mother's eyes were open very wide. But her lips were twisted and pushed together tight. It was the same kind of face Miranda made after her mother made her take cough medicine.

Miranda's mother came into the room. "You look pretty funny yourself. What are you doing up? It's way past your bedtime."

"I know *tha-at*," Miranda said. Why did grown-ups always want to tell you stuff you already knew? "I went to sleep. Then I woke up because of Grandma Helen."

"Grandma Helen," her mother echoed.

She leaned over the bed to stare into Miranda's face.

"Is that who you were talking to? Grandma Helen?"

"Uh-huh." Miranda nodded. "Mommy—"

"But you know you can't do that, right?" her mother interrupted. Her voice had a funny sound to it. The scared sound. "Miranda, sweetheart, you know Grandma Helen died three months ago."

"I know," Miranda said. "But Mommy—"

"What, sweetheart?" her mother asked.

"She's standing right behind you."

"Okay." Jason's voice rang out loud and clear over the speakerphone. "Let's do our check-in on the Johnston case. Lyssa, why don't you get us started?"

Lyssa leaned forward in her seat. She was riding with Grant and Jason in one of the SUVs. The TAPS team was on its way to investigate the Johnston home. Jen and the Hammond twins were squeezed into the equipment van.

"I talked to Mrs. Johnston last week," Lyssa began. "She was pretty upset. She said her daughter, Miranda, claims she talks to her grandmother, Helen Johnston, in her bedroom at night. Grandma Helen *died* three months ago."

"Anyone else in the family see her?" asked Jen. As usual, Jen was the first one to ask questions.

"Mrs. Johnston says she saw *something* in the hall near Miranda's room. But she wasn't sure who or what it was."

"How old is the daughter?" The voice of one of the Hammond twins came through the speaker.

"Four years old," Lyssa answered.

"Wow," Jen said. "Have we ever investigated a case with someone this young?"

"Yes, we have." Jason spoke up. "It isn't easy."

"Do you think we can *believe* her?" Jen sounded worried. Lyssa was thinking the very same question. When they got to the Johnston house, Jen would be in charge of where to place the cameras, voice recorders, and other equipment. If Miranda wasn't telling the truth, Jen could wind up wasting a lot of time.

"It's not that I think the little girl is lying," Jen said. "But sometimes little kids don't know the difference between real and make-believe."

"That's okay. Neither does Jason!" Grant joked.

Lyssa laughed out loud.

"A four-year-old having a sighting isn't as weird as you might think," said one of the twins. "We had our first sighting when we were six."

"I still can't get over the fact that you grew up in a haunted house," Lyssa said. "I'm still trying to imagine what that was like."

"Actually, it wasn't bad, it was just home to us," he replied. "I think it would be harder to move into a house and *then* find out it's haunted!"

"But when you grow up with it, you think it's normal," the second Hammond twin chimed in. "Kids accept weird stuff a lot more easily than grown-ups do."

"I never thought of it that way. That's a good point, Mark." Lyssa risked a guess about which twin was speaking.

"Mike," the voice said. "Mark is driving."

"Excuse me?" Lyssa, Jason, and Grant all yelled at the same time.

As a researcher, Mark Hammond rocked. He could always dig up weird details nobody else would even think to look for. But when it came to the day-to-day stuff, Mark's mind could wander. That made him a terrible driver!

"Calm down, everybody," Jen said through the speakerphone. "He's joking. No *way* I would ride with him. *I'm* driving." She had to shout to be heard over the twins' laughter.

"I think I see what Mike means about little kids accepting weird stuff," Jen continued when the laughter died down. "Little kids believe in Santa Claus. They think the tooth fairy leaves a quarter under their pillow at night."

"Kids are very open," Jason agreed. "Sometimes they see and hear more than adults."

"Because they don't know they're not supposed to," Lyssa added.

"That's right."

"Hey, you guys, I think we're almost there," Jen said. "We just passed the library your directions mention, Lyssa."

"Roger that," Lyssa said. "We're pulling up to the house. See you in a few. You got robbed, by the way. The tooth fairy always gave *me* a dollar!"

The whole team was laughing when Jason switched off the speakerphone.

"Thank you for coming," Mrs. Johnston said. She and her husband were sitting side by side on the couch.

Jason introduced the team to the Johnstons. Lyssa always felt proud when he called her the chief interviewer. Then Jen and the Hammond twins went outside to start unloading the equipment.

"So," Mr. Johnston said, "what happens now?"

"We'd like to speak with your daughter," Lyssa said. "She seems to be at the center of whatever is going on here."

"She's in her room," Mrs. Johnston said. "I'll take you up. Follow me."

Lyssa stood up, but Jason and Grant stayed in their chairs.

"You go ahead," Jason said. "Grant and I will stay with Mr. Johnston and take a tour of the downstairs."

"Okay." Lyssa nodded. Her heart pounded as she followed

Mrs. Johnston up the stairs. She felt fluttery. *Is there really a ghost up here?*

"Most of the sightings were upstairs, right?" she asked. Her legs felt a little shaky as they climbed the stairs.

"Yes. That's right," Mrs. Johnston said, nodding. "We sometimes hear noises in the rest of the house. But all the sightings have been in or around Miranda's room."

Lyssa and Mrs. Johnston reached the upstairs hall. Thick carpet muffled the sound of their footsteps.

"Here we are," Mrs. Johnston said. She pushed open the first door on the right.

Lyssa took a deep breath and peeked into the room. She could see a young girl sitting on a fluffy pink area rug. Miranda Johnston had the palest blond hair Lyssa had ever seen. So pale, it was almost white.

Miranda was looking down at the stuffed polar bear she held in her lap. There was a child's tea set on the rug in front of her.

"Miranda," Mrs. Johnston said. "Sweetheart, this is one of the people Daddy and I told you about. Her name is Lyssa. She wants to talk to you about Grandma Helen."

Miranda Johnston looked up. Lyssa felt a strange chill down her spine. Miranda's eyes were bright blue and shiny, like doll eyes. They seemed to glow in the light from above.

"I can't talk about Grandma Helen right now," Miranda said in a high, clear voice. "Polar Bear and I are having a tea party."

Those amazing blue eyes beamed into Lyssa's. "*You're* not invited."

Okay, Lyssa thought.

"That's all right," she said. She kept her voice friendly and cheerful. "Could I wait until you're done? I really love stuffed animals." She saw that Miranda's bed was covered with them. "Would it be okay with you if I played with them a little?" Lyssa asked.

"Which one is your favorite?" Miranda asked. "If you *could* pick one. But you can't. They're *mine*."

"This one, I think," Lyssa said. She held up an orange striped cat with long white whiskers.

"Yes! That's Henry," Miranda said. "He's my *favorite*, except for Polar Bear."

Lyssa smiled. *Way to go, Lyssa!*

Miranda lifted the bear so that his mouth was to her ear. "Okay," she said, and nodded to the bear. "I'll tell her." She put Polar Bear back down into her lap. "Polar Bear says you can come to the party. Bring Henry with you."

"Thanks, Miranda," Lyssa said. "Henry, would you like to come to a tea party?" She put the cat next to her ear. "He says he'd love to come."

Lyssa sat down across from Miranda on the fluffy pink rug.

"Henry will meow, if you squeeze him just right," Miranda explained. "Grandma Helen gave him to me. Polar Bear too.

She showed me how. But don't do it. It's not polite to meow at a tea party."

"Okay," Lyssa said. "Good to know."

For the next several minutes, she and Miranda played tea party with the stuffed animals. Miranda's mother paced back and forth near the door.

"Does Grandma Helen ever come to your tea parties?" Lyssa finally asked. She thought the timing was right. Miranda seemed comfortable with her now.

Miranda shook her head. "Not anymore." She lifted a tiny cup to Polar Bear's mouth, pretending he was taking a sip. "Not since she died."

"But she does come to see you, doesn't she?" Lyssa asked.

Miranda nodded. "Mostly, she comes at night. After Mommy and Daddy go to bed. I have to stay awake a long time. Sometimes it's really hard to keep my eyes open."

She shot a look in her mother's direction. "You're not mad, are you, Mommy? That I stay up past my bedtime?"

Mrs. Johnston shook her head. "Of course not, sweetheart."

"Do you know why Grandma Helen comes to see you?" Lyssa asked.

Lyssa knew this was a very important question. Grant and Jason said many times that ghosts are just people. Often they appear to living people because they *need* something.

If Lyssa could figure out *why* Grandma Helen returned night after night, maybe the team could decide how to help her pass on. Sometimes that's all a spirit wants. A little help to go to her rest.

Miranda shook her head. "No. I don't know why she comes. Sometimes I think she wants to tell me. But she never stays very long."

Miranda sighed. "I'm tired of playing this game," she announced. "I'm hungry. I want a snack. Chocolate graham crackers are my favorite."

She set Polar Bear down on the rug and stood up. Then she held out a hand for Lyssa. Lyssa climbed to her feet and took Miranda's hand.

"We have to go to the kitchen," the four-year-old said. "I can show you all the places I see Grandma Helen."

"But sweetheart—" Miranda's mother spoke up. "Maybe this is enough for now?"

Miranda's blue eyes flashed. "Don't be such a Little Louie Worrywart, Mommy!" she scolded.

Her mother gasped. Lyssa saw the woman's whole body shudder.

"Miranda, where did you *hear* that?" Mrs. Johnston cried. "How can you *know* that? *How?*"

"I'm sorry," Lyssa said. "What did Miranda say?"

"Little Louie Worrywart. It's a nickname Helen gave to Miranda's dad when he was a little boy. Grandma Helen and I are the only ones who know that name. There is no way Miranda could know it."

Miranda let go of Lyssa's hand and darted for the bedroom door. But when she reached it, she turned back. Her bright blue eyes grew wide.

"Of *course* I know that," Miranda said. "Grandma Helen told me."

Then she skipped through the doorway and was gone.

"Okay," Jason said. "Everybody ready to go dark?"

The team huddled together in the front hall of the house. Lyssa could see the living room and dining room to the right. The steps that led to Miranda's bedroom were dead ahead.

Dead ahead. Very funny, Lyssa, she thought.

Jason pointed at Jennifer. She flipped a wall switch.

The overhead lights in the Johnston living room went off. Lyssa blinked in the sudden darkness.

The only lights in the whole house were the flashing clock on the TV, the faint flicker of the computer monitors, and Miranda's night-light in the upstairs hall.

Miranda was asleep. Her parents were in their bedroom, trying to sleep as well.

There was silence as Lyssa's eyes slowly adjusted to the dark.

"Oh, man," Mike Hammond whispered. "I love this part."

Lyssa chuckled, then clapped a hand across her mouth. Mike was right. Going dark *was* always exciting. It meant the real reason they were here was about to start. Lyssa stood perfectly still. She tried to reach out with senses other than her eyes.

She could hear the grandfather clock in the living room. *Tick. Tick.* She heard the other team members breathing in and out. The floor overhead creaked. Footsteps? No. Lyssa knew it was just one of the noises a house makes. The refrigerator in the kitchen came on with a loud, metallic rattle.

Lyssa's skin tingled. All of her senses were *alive*.

"All right, everyone. You know the drill," Jason said in a whisper.

Lyssa let out a breath. She hadn't even realized she had been holding it in.

"Grandma Helen usually appears in Miranda's room close to midnight. If that happens tonight, the thermal camera and the motion sensors should pick it up."

"And we'll be able to see any activity on the computer monitors I set up in the dining room," Jen said.

"Okay," Grant said. "Why don't you keep an eye on that for us? Take the twins with you."

"Roger that," Jen said. "C'mon, guys."

Jen and the Hammonds walked into the dining room. Lyssa could see them from the hall. She watched Jen sit down at the table. The twins stood leaning over her shoulder. All three stared at the computer screens. The light from the screens gave their faces an eerie green glow.

Creepy, thought Lyssa.

"All right," Jason said. "I'm going to try to make contact with Helen."

He began to speak in a low, clear voice....

"My name is Jason Hawes. I am here with Grant Wilson and Lyssa Frye. We were invited here by the Johnston family to try and contact Helen Johnston.

"Helen, if you can hear me, I want you to know that your family is worried. They know you do not mean them any harm. And we do not mean to harm or upset you. But they do not know why you are here.

"Helen, are you in the house with us now? Can you give us some sign to show us you are here?"

He paused.

Silence.

The silence feels different—almost like someone is listening, Lyssa thought.

Jason nodded in her direction.

She spoke up. "Helen, this is Lyssa Frye. I have one of Miranda's stuffed animals."

She held up Henry the cat. Slowly Lyssa walked over to the stairs and set Henry on the bottom step. Then she backed away.

"Miranda says you gave Henry to her. If you're here with us, could you make Henry meow? It doesn't take much strength. I know you can do this, Helen. Miranda says you showed her how."

BANG!

The sound made Lyssa shriek. She spun around.

Bang. Bang. Bang. BANG!

"What's *that*?" she whispered. "Where's it coming from?"

"I think it's coming from the kitchen," Mark called from the dining room. He came striding out, holding his thermal camera in front of him.

A swinging door separated the kitchen from the dining room. The door was closed.

"Definitely getting something on the camera," Mark reported.

"Could just be the fridge," Mike reminded them. "A refrigerator gives off warmth that could register on the camera."

BANG! BANG! BANG! BANG!

Lyssa's heart thudded in her chest. Mark took a quick step back.

"Jay and I will go check it out," Grant said. He and Jason moved forward cautiously, walking on tiptoe.

They look like they're stalking something, Lyssa thought. *No, that's not right. They're* hunting.

Hunting ghosts.

Grant reached out and pushed open the swinging door. He

and Jason stepped through it. With a *whoosh*, the door swung closed behind them.

Grant and Jason vanished from sight.

Lyssa's skin tingled. The silence rang in her ears. The air suddenly felt heavy and damp. She stared at the kitchen door without blinking.

Listening…Waiting…

I don't want to be alone out here! Lyssa thought.

She shook off her fear and walked into the dining room. She stood beside the Hammond twins, who were still hovering around Jen's monitors.

Lyssa could see Jason and Grant on the screen now. They looked like black-and-white shadow figures. When they faced the camera, their eyes were solid white.

The banging had stopped. Lyssa could hear Jason's voice in the kitchen as he tried to make contact with Grandma Helen.

"Hey, Mike," Mark whispered. "You remember the time we thought our great-aunt Nancy came back? That's what this reminds me of. Now *that* was scary!"

"No way," Mike replied. "I thought Great-Aunt Nancy was a whole lot scarier when she was *alive!*"

"Well, Aunt Nancy did—"

"—talk more," Mike finished his sentence.

"I was going to say that," Mark said.

"I know."

"Shhhh, guys," Lyssa whispered.

"Whoa. Sorry," Mike said.

"Guys, *look*! Up there!" Lyssa pointed to the stairs. "Is it just me, or does it look brighter up there?" she whispered.

"It isn't just you," Mike replied.

Lyssa moved into the front hall. She walked slowly, holding a video camera in front of her. She sensed one of the twins moving behind her.

Lyssa could see into the living room and up the stairs to the second floor now. She stopped so abruptly that Mark bumped into her.

"Oops. Sorry," he murmured.

At the top of the stairs Lyssa could see faint greenish blue lights. They floated in the darkness above the stairs.

"Are you seeing this?" she whispered.

"Oh, yeah," Mark whispered, close behind her.

The greenish blue dots of light continued to hover. Lyssa glanced down at her camera to see how they showed up there.

Nothing. She couldn't see them on the view screen. And when she glanced up again, the glowing shapes were gone.

"That was so cool!" she cried. "I've never seen orbs before."

"Those weren't orbs. More likely plasma lights," Mark said. "Lights caused by a high energy level."

Lyssa turned to face him. "A high energy level could mean something is up there," she said.

But Mark didn't answer. He was staring straight ahead.

The back of Lyssa's neck prickled. She slowly turned around.

A figure in white stood at the top of the stairs. It seemed to hover above the top step.

Feet. I don't see any feet! Lyssa thought.

The figure started down.

One step.

Another step.

It's coming toward us!

Don't move! Lyssa told herself. *Don't run away. You're a Ghost Hunter.*

"Thirsty," the figure said in a high, clear voice. "Can I have a drink of water?"

"Of *course* you can have a drink of water, Miranda," Lyssa said. Her voice came out in a croak. *Maybe I should get a drink of water too,* she thought. Her throat was as dry as a bone.

She watched as Miranda continued down the stairs.

"Watch she doesn't trip over that nightgown," Mark warned.

Miranda's nightgown was way too long. Her mom had probably bought it for her to grow into.

That's why it looked as if she had no feet! Lyssa realized.

Lyssa moved to the bottom of the stairs and held out a hand. "Would you like to go together?" she said.

Miranda took Lyssa's hand.

"Can I have my favorite cup?" she asked.

"Why not?" Lyssa replied. The two walked toward the kitchen. "You'll have to show me which one it is."

"That's easy," Miranda said. "It has a picture of me on it. It was a present for Grandma Helen. But it's ours now because she died. She's in the spare bedroom now."

Lyssa stopped walking. *"What?"*

Miranda stopped too. She gazed up at Lyssa. In the dim light, her blue eyes looked like two shiny buttons.

"Grandma Helen is in the spare bedroom," Miranda repeated. "I saw her. Before I came down." Lyssa froze. Her mouth dropped open.

Miranda gave Lyssa a push to get her moving again. "Don't stop here. I'm thirsty," she said. "Come on."

"Hello, Miranda." Lyssa heard Grant's voice. "What are you doing up?"

"She got up for a drink of water," Lyssa replied. "She says Grandma Helen is in the upstairs spare bedroom."

Miranda let go of Lyssa's hand. "Don't *do* that," she cried, stamping her foot. "Mommy always does that, and I hate it. I can talk for myself! I was saving the most important part for last. Now I might not tell you at all."

Lyssa felt a chill sweep over her. Did she just make a big mistake? Did she ruin the team's best chance to find out what Grandma Helen wanted?

"You're right. I hate that too," she said softly. "I'm sorry."

Miranda refused to look at Lyssa.

"What were you going to tell me?" Lyssa asked.

Miranda remained silent.

"Does it have something to do with Grandma Helen?" Lyssa whispered.

Miranda lifted her eyes to meet Lyssa's gaze but said nothing.

"Are we still friends?" Lyssa asked again.

Miranda nodded.

"Good. I'm so glad," Lyssa said.

Miranda twisted a lock of hair around her finger. Then finally she said: "Grandma Helen wants it. She told me she won't go away until she finds it. Can I have my drink of water now?"

The rest of the night was quiet. Grant decided to pack up the equipment at dawn. Then he and Jason sent the team home to get some sleep.

The plan: to meet back at the TAPS office at 14:00 hours—two o'clock.

"Okay," Grant said when everyone gathered again. "Are you ready to go over the evidence?"

The team members sat around the oval table in the conference room, once a big bedroom, at the back of the house.

"Can we start with the audio from Miranda's room?" Lyssa asked.

"Sure," Jen said with a smile. "I think we're all eager to find out what happened in Miranda's room right before she came downstairs."

Jen clicked on the digital recorder in front of her on the table. "Okay. Here we go."

At first, there was no sound at all. Then Lyssa could hear little things. Sounds that probably meant Miranda was rolling over in bed. Maybe even sitting up.

Then, all of a sudden, they heard Miranda's soft whisper.

"Grandma, is that you?"

"We can hear so clearly," Lyssa murmured. "Downstairs, I couldn't hear a sound."

"The equipment is super-sensitive," Jen said.

"Why can't you talk to me, like you did the first time?" Miranda's voice, a little louder on the tape. *"Why can't you tell me what you want?"*

And then…a second voice. It seemed to creep in, like fog, like smoke.

A whisper barely loud enough to be heard. Lyssa leaned closer. She held her breath.

This is real. I'm not imagining it, she thought. *I am listening to the voice of a ghost!*

"*What?*" said Miranda's voice. "*I can't understand you, Grandma Helen. Say it again. Say it louder this time.*"

Again came the ghostly whisper. So soft…as if from far away.

"What's she saying?" Lyssa cried in frustration. "I can't make it out."

That's when she heard it clearly.

"*…Find it!*" whispered the ghost.

"Did everyone else hear that?" Lyssa asked. Her voice trembled. She glanced around the room, searching the faces of the others. Everybody nodded.

"Play it again, please, Jen," Jason said.

"Will do." Jen nodded.

"*Why can't you talk to me, like you did the first time?*" came Miranda's voice again. "*Why won't you tell me what you want?*"

"*Find it. Find it. Find it.*"

The ghostly whisper seemed to fill the whole room.

At a nod from Jason, Jen turned off the sound.

"Whoa!" Lyssa exclaimed. "That totally gave me goose bumps! That *has* to be Grandma Helen, right?"

She turned to Grant. "*Find it?* Does that mean Grandma Helen lost something? What? How will we know?"

"We'll ask her," Grant replied. "But I think we'll need a little extra help."

"Good idea. I was just about to go there," Jason said.

"I wish you'd let the rest of us know what you mean," Mark said.

"I'm thinking of calling in Bethany Lane," Jason said. "She's been very helpful in other cases like this."

"Good call," Grant replied.

"Who's Bethany Lane?" Jen asked.

"She's a sensitive," Grant explained. "Someone who reaches out to spirits. We've worked with her before, and she helped us get some valuable evidence. She would be perfect for this case."

Jason stood up. "Okay," he said. "I'll go call her."

"Do you really think she can reach Grandma Helen?" Lyssa asked.

Jason raised his hands. He had his fingers crossed on both of them.

A week later, Bethany Lane and Miranda were sitting side by side on Miranda's bed. Lyssa stood with Jason, Grant, and Miranda's parents in the doorway.

Lyssa saw why Grant thought Bethany was such a good choice. She was just about the same age as Grandma Helen. And it was clear that Miranda liked her right away.

Bethany had a good sense of humor. She was wearing a T-shirt with the letters *O I C U* on it. Even Miranda thought that was funny.

"Okay," Bethany said. "Everybody understands what I'm about to do, right?" Bethany looked down at Miranda. "How about you, Miranda? Do you understand?"

"Of course I do," Miranda answered in her direct way. "You're going to try to talk to Grandma Helen."

"That's right. I am." Bethany nodded. "And I'm going to try to help *her* talk to *you*. I'm going to start by making a noise with these two stones."

She lifted a pair of shiny gray stones from her lap. They were egg shaped and fit inside her palms.

"The sound the stones make will change the energy in the room," Bethany explained. "This makes it easier for some spirits to talk to us. I'm hoping they will help Grandma Helen."

She glanced around the room. "If everybody is ready, I'll begin."

"We're ready," Miranda's father said. "Go ahead."

Bethany stretched her arms out in front of her. Then she made a quick move and banged the two stones together. She made it look as if she was clashing a pair of cymbals together.

Clack. The stones connected with a sharp sound. Bethany struck the stones together twice more. *Clack. Clack.* After the third strike, she called out in a loud voice:

"I'm trying to reach the spirit of Helen Johnston. If you're in this room, will you give us a sign?"

Lyssa shivered. The room suddenly felt cold. As if a strong breeze had blown in.

Temperature drop!

Bethany asked for a sign—and Helen gave her one. A temperature drop can mean a spirit has come near.

Lyssa shivered. Her skin tingled. Would this work? Were they really going to talk to Grandma Helen?

Was she in the room with them right now?

Lyssa turned to Miranda. She was sitting perfectly still at Bethany's side. Her blue eyes darted around the room.

Lyssa knew she was looking for Grandma Helen.

"Thank you, Helen," Bethany said. "We're all very glad you decided to join us. I'm going to tell you the truth, Helen. We need your help. We know there's something you want us to do. There is something you need before you can rest."

Bethany paused. The room was silent. Lyssa could hear the wind outside the bedroom window. Bethany spoke again. "Can you tell us what it is, Helen? Can you help us help *you*?"

Without warning, Miranda uttered a groan. She turned her head quickly from side to side, as if searching for something.

Mrs. Johnston stepped toward her. "Miranda, baby…" she began.

"Mommy! Stop talking!" Miranda cried. "I don't want to listen to you. I want to listen to Grandma Helen."

Mrs. Johnston pressed her hands against her mouth. Her eyes were huge with fear. She took her husband's hand and held on to it tightly.

Suddenly Miranda shot off the bed as though she had been pushed from behind.

"I'm going," she cried. "I'm going."

Miranda dashed out into the hall. She raced down the stairs. Lyssa and Bethany were right behind her. Miranda's parents came next, with Jason and Grant last of all.

THWACK!

Miranda hit the swinging door between the dining room and kitchen with both hands. It crashed back against the kitchen counter. She kept right on going.

At the far end of the room, Miranda came to a stop in front of another door. Lyssa and Bethany stepped up behind her.

Miranda pointed to the door. Then she looked up at Lyssa and took her by the hand. Her fingers were ice cold.

"The basement. We have to go down there."

Lyssa reached out and opened the door. In front of her stretched a steep flight of wooden stairs.

Miranda started forward. She moved so quickly, Lyssa almost tumbled into the stairwell.

Lyssa tightened her hold on Miranda's hand. She made her stop on the top step.

"Wait a minute, Miranda," she said. "I can't see where I'm going."

But Miranda pulled forward with surprising strength. *It's almost as if she's being pulled down there,* Lyssa thought with a chill of fear.

"There's a light switch on the wall to your left," Mrs. Johnston called from the kitchen.

With her free hand, Lyssa fumbled for the light switch.

Miranda tugged. "Come on, Lyssa," she said. *"Come on."* Lyssa's fingers finally found the switch. She flipped it and the lights came on.

Miranda yanked so hard on her hand that Lyssa had to grab the banister to keep from falling. She let the little girl drag her down the stairs. Everyone else followed with their feet clattering against the wood. Halfway across the basement, Miranda stopped. She sagged against Lyssa's legs as if she was all worn out.

"She's gone," Miranda whimpered. "Grandma Helen is gone."

"Wait." Grant came quickly down the stairs. He pointed to some cardboard boxes on the floor at Miranda's feet. "What's in those boxes?" he asked.

Mr. Johnston answered, "Nothing much. Just some stuff I've been meaning to throw out."

"Could any of the items in the boxes be Helen's?" Jason picked up on Grant's thought.

"Let me see," Miranda's father said. He lifted a flap on one of the boxes. "Yes, I think some of this was my mother's."

"Do you think what she's looking for is in there?" Lyssa asked.

"Let's look, Daddy," Miranda said.

After nearly an hour of searching, Miranda and her dad found several things that belonged to Grandma Helen. But nothing that seemed valuable or important.

Then Miranda's dad reached way down deep into one of the boxes and found an old cigar box. "I think this may be what my mother is looking for," he said. He cradled the box in his hands.

"I remember seeing this box when I was a little boy," Mr. Johnston continued. "I think it belonged to my father. You see, I never knew my father. He died right after I was born. My mom never married again. She wore her wedding ring until the day she died."

He let out a whoosh of air. "But she used to talk about another ring. She said it wasn't very valuable. Dad won it in a game at a carnival. But Mom always had a soft spot for that ring. It was my father's first gift to her.

"Maybe that ring is what she wants," he said. "I think it's in this box."

"Open it, Daddy," Miranda said. Her eyes were bright and shining.

Carefully, Mr. Johnston lifted the top of the cigar box. He flipped back the lid.

"Let me see," Miranda demanded. "Is it there? Are you right?"

"It's there," her father said. Lyssa saw that he had tears in his eyes. Mrs. Johnston went to stand beside her family. Mr. Johnston took the ring out of the box and held it up. The tiny stone flashed, just once, as it caught the basement light.

"It's beautiful," Mrs. Johnston said softly. "But I think your mom was wrong about one thing. That ring *is* valuable."

"Yes, you're right." Mr. Johnston put an arm around his wife's shoulders. Miranda stood between them, leaning against her parents' legs. "It's valuable to Mom. So valuable she didn't want to leave it behind."

"So what do we do now?" Mrs. Johnston asked.

"Well," Mr. Johnston answered, "I have an idea."

When he told everyone what it was, Miranda smiled.

Two days later, Lyssa stood in a graveyard.

The entire TAPS team, including Bethany Lane, joined the Johnston family at Helen Johnston's graveside.

Grandma Helen's grave was underneath a big maple tree. The tree's leaves rustled in the late-afternoon breeze.

It's pretty here, Lyssa thought. *Peaceful.*

"I'm glad you convinced the caretaker to let you do this," Bethany said.

"I'm glad too," said Mr. Johnston. "This feels right, some-how."

"Things still quiet at home?" Lyssa asked him.

Mr. Johnston nodded. "Things have been quiet ever since we found the ring. I'm certain this is what my mother has been looking for."

He turned to Miranda. "All set, sweetheart?"

Miranda nodded.

"Then let's do this," her father said.

He and Miranda got down on their hands and knees. At the base of Helen's headstone was a hole about the size of a quarter. Not very big around, but deep.

The Johnston family wanted to give the ring back to Grandma Helen.

Mr. Johnston placed the cigar box beside his mother's grave-stone. He opened the box and let Miranda take out the ring. It was wrapped in sparkly pink tissue paper.

"Go ahead, honey," Mr. Johnston said.

Biting her lower lip in concentration, Miranda leaned over and dropped the ring into the hole.

"There you go, Grandma Helen. We're giving you your ring," she said. "Now you can rest."

"Yes. Rest in peace," Lyssa said.

The
GHOST HUNT
Guide

by
Jason Hawes and
Grant Wilson

Introduction

Have you ever walked down a dark hallway all alone but had the feeling that someone was there with you? Someone you couldn't see? Have you heard voices in the night coming from your own closet? Or have you seen something you can't explain—a flash of light or a shadow that comes from nowhere?

If you've had experiences like these or if you are interested in finding out for yourself if the paranormal is real . . .

THIS *GHOST HUNT* GUIDE IS FOR YOU.

The *Ghost Hunt* Guide has tons of information and tips that we have picked up in our TAPS investigations. The guide shares our best advice and our methods, and it explains the tools we use. You can be a ghost hunter, too! It doesn't always take the high-tech gadgets that we use on television.

Are you ready to find out how? As we always say: Let's rock and roll!

—JASON HAWES AND GRANT WILSON

THE
TAPS
METHOD

The very first thing we do before any investigation is to get permission from the person who owns the house or location. You should also get permission from your parent or guardian before any ghost hunt, so they can make sure the place is safe for you to investigate in the dark.

People call us ghost hunters, but eight times out of ten, we don't find ghosts. Most of the time, we find logical reasons for the strange sounds and unusual sightings people report. And that's fine with us.

Of course, it is exciting when we *do* find evidence of the paranormal. How do we do it? We have a secret method. **When we investigate a site, we try to prove that the place is NOT haunted.** We try to find logical reasons for the spooky things people tell us about the house we're investigating.

If someone feels a cold draft in a room without a window, we look for a loose wall panel that lets the cold air in.

If someone reports banging in the night, we examine the pipes. Old pipes often make banging sounds.

We call these reports of noises and visions **claims**. And when we can prove that the claims are not paranormal, we say we have **debunked the claims**.

We always start out by trying to debunk the claims. We want to be absolutely sure that we have looked at every logical explanation. Then we can say that something paranormal is going on. We want to be scientific and examine the evidence. As Jason once said:

"If you set out to prove a haunting, anything will seem like evidence. If you set out to *disprove* it, you'll end up with only those things you can't explain away."

Every TAPS investigation follows the same steps:

1. **The Interview**

2. **The Sweep**

3. **Setting Up the Command Center and the Equipment**

4. **Collecting Evidence**

5. **Research**

6. **Analyzing the Evidence**

7. **Conclusions**

Follow us, and we'll take you through it step-by-step.

STEP 1:
THE
INTERVIEW

Your friend Dana says she and her sister, Jen, hear sounds at night. And sometimes when Dana wakes up, some of the objects in her room have been moved. Great! You're ready to investigate her house, right? No, not yet.

First you have to get more information about what she has seen and heard. You have to find out more about the claims, and we do this by asking a lot of questions. You have to get the complete story. This is what we call the interview.

Here are some of the questions you might want to ask Dana and Jen:

- When was the first time you heard these sounds?
- Where exactly were you?
- What did you hear?
- Did you both hear the same thing?
- Did you recognize any words?
- What did you do?
- Did you call anyone else into the room?
- Did they hear anything?
- Did it sound like a human voice?
- Did the voice sound like a man or a woman? Or did it sound like a child?

- Did you talk to the spirit? What did you say?
- Did it react to anything you said or did?
- When did you first notice that an object in your room was moved?
- What was it?
- Does this happen every night?
- Are the same objects moved? Or do they change?
- Have you seen anything in the room? What did it look like?
- Where exactly did you see it?
- Have there been any sounds or sightings in other parts of the house? Where?

When was the first time you heard these sounds?

Where exactly were you?

What did you hear?

Did you both hear the same thing?

Did you recognize any words?

What did you do?

Did you call anyone else into the room?

Did they hear anything?

Did it sound like a human voice?

Did the voice sound like a man or a woman?

Or did it sound like a child?

The answers to these questions will tell you where to begin your investigation. They will tell you where the "hot spots" are—in other words, the places where spooky stuff happened.

If all the activity has been in Dana's room, you will look over that room carefully. Later, that's where you'll want to put your cameras and recorders.

Sometimes the interview gives you a clue about why the spirit is there. Remember the Grandma Helen case? Miranda told us that her grandmother wanted something, and she was right.

Sometimes you can find a logical explanation of what is really happening. We once interviewed a woman who was seeing frightening dark shadows. In the interview we learned that the woman was taking a new medicine. It turned out that the medicine was causing her to see the dark shadows. We were able to make her feel better—not only by proving that her house wasn't haunted but also by having her medicine changed. That case was a win!

Interviews can be very helpful for finding out if someone is not telling the truth. If you keep asking fact questions—like the ones on the list we gave you earlier—and the answers keep changing, someone may be trying to trick you. Hey, it happens to all of us.

STEP 2:
THE
SWEEP

At TAPS we do most of our investigations at night. That's because spirits seem to appear most often at night. Also, the evidence we find is shadowy or has a faint light. The best way to find these strange things is to get rid of all the light. Then we use special infrared cameras that can see in the dark.

Still, we always begin our investigation during the day with a complete tour of the site. If you see the place in daylight, you are less likely to bump into something or stumble at night. Knowing where you are is the first step to a good night of ghost hunting.

But there's another reason. We want to find logical explanations for the weird noises or events at the site. We call this the sweep because we want to clear out things that seem like paranormal evidence— but aren't. **We look for what we call false positives. That's our expression for things that look paranormal but aren't.**

The daytime is a good time to look for debunking evidence. You don't have to be plumbers like us to find reasons for "the unexplainable." If you look closely, you will be able to debunk lots of claims. Debunking claims can be almost as much fun as finding paranormal activity! The members of TAPS certainly have a good time doing it.

Use this handy checklist to help you when you walk through your site.

SITE SWEEP CHECKLIST

Be sure to look closely for these things:

- **old pipes** can make scary noises
- **radiators** can make steam and make whistling sounds
- **water leaks** can cause noises and creepy dampness
- **air ducts** can carry voices and create "woo" sounds
- **a house settling** can make creaky sounds and can make floors uneven, which can result in falls or weird feelings
- **natural expansion of wood or other building materials** can cause squeaks and groans
- **mice, rats, raccoons, and other critters**—even termites in the walls—cause noise and scratching, and they can move in the dark
- **cracks in windows** create drafts and drops in temperature
- **blinds or shades that blow in the wind** can make banging noises
- **bad insulation** can create a cold spot on a wall

STEP 3:
SETTING UP THE COMMAND CENTER AND THE EQUIPMENT

Before we "go dark," we have to set up. We put cameras and recorders in the hot spots (the places where strange sounds and sights have happened). We decide where each member of the team will be. And most important, we set up our **Central Command Center**.

The Central Command Center is where the team can meet and regroup during the night. On a TAPS investigation we set up monitors so the team members can check out the action in other parts of the house. We can also see where the other team members are.

Your ghost hunt isn't going to be as complicated as ours, but it is still very important to set up a command center. Your team has to know where to go. They need to remember that they are part of a team. You don't want them getting so interested in their own recordings or photos that they forget to focus on the team's goal.

STEP 4:
COLLECTING
EVIDENCE

You've done your interview. You know the claims. You've toured the site. You've set up your command center. Now you're ready to use your equipment to see if you can find some ghosts.

We use lots of cool equipment at TAPS. But you can have a totally cool investigation if you have just these basic items:

audio recorder

video recorder

camera

compass

flashlight and lots of batteries

digital thermometer (Note: Use

an ambient thermometer — one that

measures the room temperature.)

But mostly you need your eyes, your ears, and your brain. There are some things that no equipment can record. We have experienced phantom smells. We've had the feeling of being touched by a spirit. We've felt a cool wind come up suddenly. These experiences have helped us learn what is paranormal. They have also taught us to understand the spirits themselves.

As we always say, ghosts are people, too, so they think like people. They think like you, because they *are* like you. That's why no equipment will ever be as important as your brain and your senses.

GHOST HUNTING EQUIPMENT

The equipment TAPS uses are the same tools that scientists use.

EMF Detector: This measures the force given off by electrical charges. Scientists call this force the electromagnetic field. We use the detector to see if there is a sudden increase in the electromagnetic field, which could mean a spirit has entered the area. **You can use a compass.** If there is a sudden change in the electromagnetic field, the needle will spin around. There is another reason we use an EMF detector. Some people are very sensitive to electromagnetic fields. A strong electromagnetic field can make them feel sick or dizzy. Sometimes it gives people a creepy feeling, which makes them think there are paranormal things happening. When we find high EMFs we often tell people to have an electrician fix the electricity in the house. Sometimes the creepy feelings go away, and we can debunk the claim.

Audio Recorder: We use this to record sounds at the site. Some of the most important evidence we get is from sounds we record.

Digital Ambient Thermometer: We use this to measure changes in the temperature of the room. A drop in temperature can mean a spirit has entered the room.

DV Camcorder: A digital video camera is used to record video of the investigation.

IR Camera: A camera that uses infrared to see in the dark. Our eyes can't see infrared light waves, but the camera can use them to make pictures.

Thermal Camera: A special kind of IR camera. Thermal cameras collect visual information about heat and cold. They make warmth and coldness visible. We use them to detect cold spots and warm spots—and to watch for changes in temperature, which could mean a spirit has entered a room.

K-II Meter: Like the EMF detector, this detects the electromagnetic field. A light blinks to show how strong the field is. TAPS teams have tried using K-II meters to communicate with spirits. We ask yes-or-no questions. If the spirit wishes to answer "yes," it can use energy to change the magnetic field and cause the light to blink. If the answer is "no," the light stays off.

Geophone: Scientists use this device to study earthquakes. A geophone detects vibrations. We use it to try to pick up the vibrations made when spirits walk.

GATHERING AUDIO EVIDENCE

It's night and you're ready to investigate. Your friend Justin has told you that he hears strange sounds in his house. He says it sounds like a woman crying. Sometimes he thinks he almost can make out words, but he isn't sure. He has heard this sound upstairs—in a hallway and in the small guest room.

You want to record this evidence so you can study it later. Any kind of audio recorder is useful: cassette, digital, or even a phone with a mic.

- **If you can, set up several recorders throughout a site. If possible, also carry an audio recorder around with you during the investigation.**
- **Ghost hunters like connecting an external microphone to the recorder. That way you don't confuse the sound of the recorder with sounds in the room.**

As you go through the house you will hear all sorts of normal sounds. Every sound—even something as small as a cough—must be tagged. To "tag" a sound means to say into the recorder what it is. You speak into the microphone and say, *Matt just coughed*, because when you listen to the audio later, you may not remember that your partner coughed. You may think the cough is a ghostly growl. Tagging it will clear up any confusion.

- **How do you get spirits to talk? You start by talking to them.**

Introduce yourself. Be respectful. Remember, spirits were once human and deserve the same respect as living people. Don't start off by asking how they died. Would this be the first thing *you'd* want to hear in a conversation? Ask simple and direct questions, such as "Who are you?" "What are you doing here?" or "What do you want?" Between each question wait ten to twenty seconds so the spirit has time to gather enough energy to respond. If you are lucky, you will hear the sound and be able to record it. But even if you don't hear it, you might pick up an **EVP**.

EVP is short for Electronic Voice Phenomena. These are the recorded sounds or voices of spirits. The strange thing about EVPs is that they can be heard on a recorder but not at the site by our ears.

We often rely on EVPs as evidence. Many times we have played an EVP to a client, and they have been able to recognize a phrase that was familiar to them.

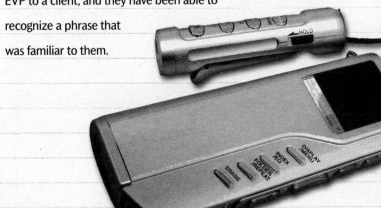

GATHERING VIDEO EVIDENCE

If you have seen us on TV, you know that we use video cameras to document our investigations. Luckily, video and digital cameras are not as expensive as they used to be. So you will probably be able to use video in your investigation.

The camcorder is a great tool. When you play back what you shot you can see everything that is happening second-by-second. You can even slow time down to study every single part of an important moment. This helps when you're not sure of what you're looking at. Is it an orb? Or just a bug flying around?

We put camcorders in hot spots we want to watch. We also use handheld cameras so the team can walk around. If possible, using a mix of both handheld cameras and camcorders is the best way to go.

Another great advantage of using a camcorder is night vision. Most DV camcorders have a night vision function. Definitely cool!

Professional ghost hunters like us also use thermal infrared (IR for short) cameras. These cameras make cold and heat visible. Using one of these IR cameras, TAPS was able to capture one of the most startling pieces of evidence we've ever collected—an image of a full-bodied apparition at Arizona's famously haunted Crescent Hotel.

Thermal cameras are also really useful in debunking a site. Let's say you're standing in a dark basement, asking a spirit to show a sign. Suddenly, you hear a rustling sound. This might seem like a paranormal experience. Then the thermal camera sees that there are mice scuttling in and out of the wall. Sometimes small critters can make pretty loud noises.

You can also use cameras that take still photographs. We don't use them very often. But if you can't borrow a camcorder to shoot video, a photo can be useful evidence. You just have to be careful. Strange images sometimes show up in a photograph. Often these images are not proof of something paranormal. It's easy to be fooled. You think you are looking at a picture of a ghost, but it's only a puff of smoke caught on film.

OTHER WAYS TO GATHER INFORMATION

One of the first pieces of equipment TAPS uses at a site is the **EMF detector** (electromagnetic field detector). An EMF detector measures the force given off by electrical charges.

Lots of things create electromagnetic fields. Power lines and electrical outlets . . . even your refrigerator. We use the EMF detector to try to find out if a spirit is in the area. The idea is that spirits are made of a type of energy that can cause changes in the natural electromagnetic field of an area. A TAPS team walks through the site with the EMF detector. What they look for is a spike in the EMF reading. That spike could mean a spirit has entered the room.

You can buy EMF detectors online, but you can also use a compass and get the same results. If there is a change in the electromagnetic field, a compass needle will spin around. You just have to make sure there are no metal items or magnets nearby.

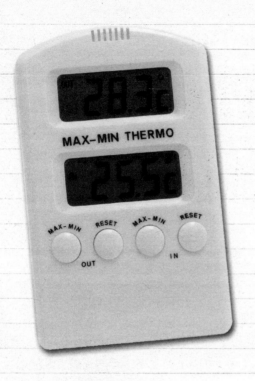

A **digital thermometer** is another common tool you can use in your ghost hunts. It is used in the search for warm spots or cold spots. A cold spot might mean that a spirit is trying to show itself and is pulling energy from the room. Of course, once you find a cold spot, the next thing you should look for is a natural cause—like a crack in a window.

It is a good idea to have a notebook and pen so you can record your readings. If you have walkie-talkies, they can be useful for keeping in touch with your teammates. We have to say it again . . . your eyes, ears, and brains are your most important tools.

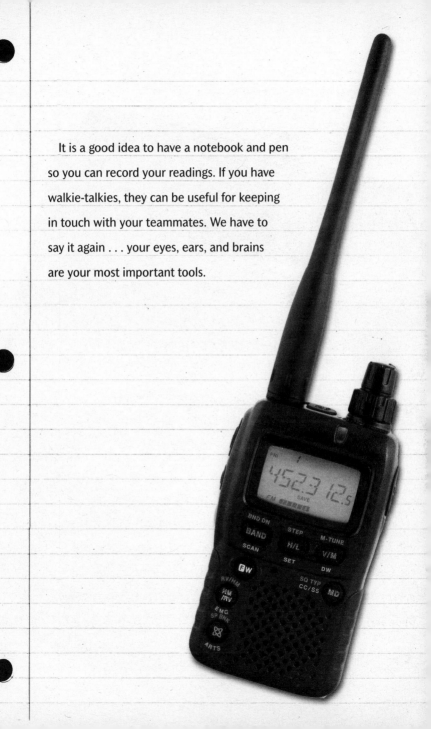

STEP 5:
RESEARCH

Doing research about the site is very important. The TAPS team spends a lot of time in libraries and on the computer looking up the history of our sites. We try to find out who lived in the house and what they did there, and we try to find out who died in the house.

Remember "Ghosts with No Legs"? That case was all about the research. Great stuff, but here's the *Ghost Hunt* tip about research:

- **Always do the research after you've investigated the site itself.**

Here's why: Did someone ever say to you, "Stand over there and try not to think of a bear?" Try it. You won't be able to do it. The idea of a bear is already in your mind. The same thing can happen in an investigation. If you show up at a site knowing that a Civil War soldier died in that house, you will have that idea in your head. Next thing you know, every shadow or flash of light will look like a soldier to you. Or you may be so busy trying to find a soldier that you will miss an important piece of evidence that has nothing to do with the Civil War.

To be a good ghost hunter you have to observe and make notes about what you observe. You can draw your conclusions later. That's when the research really helps.

STEP 6: ANALYZING THE EVIDENCE

So you have hours of video and audiotapes. You've recorded everything. Maybe you even saw some freaky phenomena first-hand. What next?

Now it's time to study and analyze the evidence. Here are some tips to help you.

Analyzing Photographs

Be very careful about photographs. Is that white blob an orb (a ball of energy caused by a spirit)? Look closely. It could be caused by any of these things:

- cold breath
- smoke
- dust
- a finger over the lens
- camera straps in front of the lens
- rain
- a lens flare
- bugs

It's not easy even for experts to be sure about orbs. A speck of dust can reflect light from a flash and make it appear several times brighter than it actually is. Most orbs are dust, bugs, moisture, and reflected light. Even if you take two pictures in a row, one that shows the "orb" and one without, this does not prove that the orb is real. It only proves that in one of the pictures, the dust was at the right angle to show up on film.

A true orb is usually whitish-blue or green and looks almost as if someone tossed a Ping-Pong ball into the picture. But even then, orbs are not ghosts. They are just blobs of energy. And there can be lots of reasons for why they are there.

Analyzing Video Evidence

Video evidence can be very convincing, but it can fool you, too. Here are some tips that will help:

Never fast-forward during the first viewing. Yes, there are hours and hours of video to watch. Yes, it will be boring. Yes, there is a large chance that you will not find any evidence of the paranormal or ghosts. But do you really want to take the chance of missing something? A hugely important piece of evidence might only be present in your footage for half a second. There's no way you would spot it if you were fast-forwarding.

Watch out for an out-of-focus picture. Some cameras, especially in dark situations, lose focus. This can make objects blurry. Blurry objects can look spooky. Is that a ghost hunched over in the background, or just a lamp? You could be fooled if the camera is out of focus.

Beware of matrixing. You may not know the word, but matrixing is something we all do. Ever look at a cloud and think it looks like your dog? How about the Man in the Moon? It's human nature to make things seem familiar and understandable. But matrixing can be a problem for ghost hunters. Let's say we have a photograph of a mysterious face in a window. We have to be sure that our minds aren't turning a random pattern of raindrops into a face.

The best way to avoid matrixing is to be aware that it's a problem. You can train yourself out of doing it. Matrixing often happens when you have a cluttered setting. Pictures of tree branches or leaves, a messy closet, fields, a mirror, or any other "busy" picture is a perfect place for matrixing to crop up. For example, if it looks as though there's a ghost crouching in the bushes next to your house in a picture, you must make sure that the image of the ghost is not the leaves or the shadows or the branches. If a ghostly image is real, the spirit will be made up of its own material.

Matrixing can occur just as easily in an audio recording as in a photograph. You might listen to the same loop of a recording a hundred times and not be entirely sure what you're hearing. You might think to yourself, "Is that a child's voice saying 'help me,' or is it just the thermostat kicking on?" This is where tagging is so helpful. Maybe you've tagged in the recording itself that the thermostat did turn on. Then you can debunk the noise. If there's no other explanation, maybe it is a real EVP. That will be decided when you get to the very last step of your investigation.

STEP 7:
CONCLUSIONS

The best way to be sure your evidence is real is to work with your team. You need people with different opinions and different sets of eyes and ears. It's important not to count anyone out. If one person disagrees with you about the evidence, it could give you a whole new way of thinking. That's why we discuss all the evidence with the whole team.

For example, in a TAPS investigation, we don't conclude that an EVP is real unless the group agrees on what we hear. We listen to the information brought up by the research. We go through all the claims that we debunked. And once everyone has been heard from, we come to our conclusions. Then we decide if we have found enough evidence to say this investigation showed real paranormal activity.

Now that you have the secret tips from the *Ghost Hunt* team, you are ready for your first test case. Turn the page and get ready to test your ghost hunting skills.

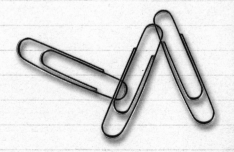

TEST YOUR GHOST HUNTING SKILLS

You are about to see how much you have learned about real ghost hunting. In this test case, you will do your own investigation. Is there really a ghost in the basement? You will analyze the evidence and come to your own conclusions. Read each question. Decide which of the choices is the right one. Then when you are finished, compare your answers with the answers at the end of this guide. Good luck!

It's a late October evening. You and your best friend, Tom, have just finished watching the season finale of *Ghost Hunters* on the old TV in your basement, and you are having a discussion about the creepy things you saw on the show. Suddenly, the light starts flickering and then flashes off. A second later, you both hear a low, sad moaning.

You and Tom race out of the basement and up the stairs to the kitchen. After catching your breath, you look at each other and know you have the same thought: "We *need* to investigate this."

First things first. You gather the digital camera, tape recorder, walkie-talkies, flashlight, and thermometer that you have in the house and set them out on the kitchen table. This will be your central command center.

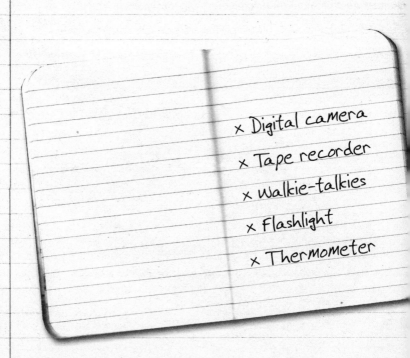

× Digital camera
× Tape recorder
× Walkie-talkies
× Flashlight
× Thermometer

1. **Now that you have everything assembled, what should you do?**

a) **Record the time and nature of the events**

b) **Start snapping pictures**

c) **Turn off all the lights in the house**

d) **Start asking the ghost questions**

Tom decides it's too scary to go back down to the basement just yet. He wants to stay in the kitchen. So you set your walkie-talkies to the same frequency, and then you head back downstairs.

2. The light switch is not working, so you turn on the flashlight. The next thing you do is . . .

a) Set up the tape recorder
b) Check to make sure the bulb is not burned out
c) Call Tom down and start a séance
d) Turn off the TV

After changing the lightbulb, you take a look around the basement. The light switch now works perfectly, so you know it wasn't an electrical problem. Still you feel a little strange. There's something weird in the air. And what about the moaning sound? You think of all the places it could have come from—maybe the water heater or the window. You listen carefully for a similar sound, or a gust of wind, but there's nothing. So you decide the next thing to do is to try to collect an EVP. You turn the light back off and set up the tape recorder. Luckily you have an external microphone attachment, so you don't have to worry about the internal noises of the recorder.

3.   **You say the date, time, and place into the recorder. What's the next thing you say?**

a)   **Why did you burn out the light bulb?**
b)   **Ghost, show me another sign by moving the couch.**
c)   **When did you die, and how did it happen?**
d)   **Who are you?**

You ask questions for about ten minutes. Although you haven't heard any responses, you still feel something is present. Finally you say, "Show me a sign." And right then you hear that moan again. This is pretty freaky, but you keep a cool head. The moan seems to be coming from the far wall. As you walk toward it, you get an unexpected chill in one spot. You think it might be a cold spot, so you use the walkie-talkie to ask Tom to bring the thermometer downstairs. After some convincing, he finally says okay.

When you take the temperature, you do find a drop in the reading in one spot. You measure nearby areas, and the temperature is much warmer. Tom snaps a few pictures to examine later and continues walking toward the wall to investigate the sounds.

The moaning gets even louder. You also notice some other faint noises mixed in with it. Then Tom notices an air conditioning vent. You realize that it goes straight up to the living room, and then you remember there's a creaky door that leads to that room.

4. **You set the recorder right next to the vent. What happens now is up to you. What do you do?**

a) **Wait to collect EVPs**

b) **Go up to the living room and experiment with the door to see if you can reproduce the noise**

c) **Take the temperature of the vent**

d) **Take a picture of the vent**

Following some experimentation, the noise stops, and both you and Tom agree that it's *possible* that the moaning was the sound of a creaking door coming through the vent. But you can't be sure. You think it's a good idea to take some more audio recordings and pictures of the basement. Tom then investigates the area around the cold spot more carefully. He looks for drafts or anything else that might explain the temperature difference. The temperature has gone back to normal, so Tom can't find an answer. He definitely thinks the air conditioning vent has nothing to do with this particular phenomenon. It's October, so the air conditioner definitely isn't on. And if it were leaking cold air into the room, he would still feel it.

Tom feels as though all you've collected so far is a handful of questions. He wants more evidence, and you agree. Quickly you grab your camping compass from your backpack and walk slowly around the basement. You make sure there is nothing metal or magnetic around. First, you move along the walls, then you near the cold spot, and finally you check the middle of the room.

5.   What will the compass tell you?

a)   The compass needle will point directly to the ghost

b)   The compass needle will point south instead of north, showing that a ghost is present

c)   The compass needle will spin around, indicating that a spirit may be changing the electromagnetic field

d)   The compass needle will point to the nearest graveyard

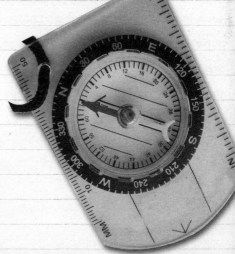

Nothing happens to the compass. No matter where you walk, it always points north. A little let down, you hand it over to Tom. He places the compass on a shelf on a wooden cabinet. The compass needle immediately starts spinning crazily back and forth. He calls you over to look.

"I don't like this. Look at the needle move!" he says. "What if it's a mean ghost?"

"Relax," you say. You move the compass left, then right. As you move it, the needle moves in the opposite direction, toward the spot where it was spinning around. You point out to Tom that there's an electrical outlet underneath the cabinet.

"It's only electricity," you say. "No ghosts in the walls here. This isn't evidence; the compass is just reacting to the wires. I think we've done just about all we can here. What should we do now?"

Tom suggests interviewing your parents. Maybe they've experienced something similar that might help the investigation, or they might have an idea about why the light went out. You round everybody up and reconvene at the central command center. You ask questions about the building of the house, and you ask if there was ever any trouble with the wiring. Nothing comes to anyone's mind. Tom asks about the moaning sound. No one has an answer.

Your dad brushes it off, saying your minds were playing tricks on you. But your mom seems a little less eager to dismiss what happened. She mentions a chest of old clothes that was in the basement when they moved into the house years ago. The clothes have been down there ever since. For some reason she just never got rid of them.

You think maybe the spirit could be attached to the clothes—that maybe when the spirit was alive, the clothes belonged to it. You and Tom go back down and check out the chest. It's pretty close to where the cold spot was. You take a picture of the chest, which is pushed into a closet where your family's winter coats hang. Tom makes one last attempt to get an EVP.

"Spirit, if those clothes belonged to you, please say something now."

A few seconds later, Tom turns off the microphone. You both decide that you've collected enough evidence and that it's time to draw the investigation to a close. It's near midnight, and you need to get some sleep to go over the data in the morning.

When you wake up, you decide to first listen to the audio for EVPs. You listen carefully with headphones, but you don't hear any suspicious noises, just the regular sounds of the basement . . . until you get to the part where Tom asks his last question. Right after Tom asks about the clothes, there's a faint sound, sort of like the moan you heard the night before. You turn the volume all the way up and listen again. It sounds like a voice saying "my jacket." You play the recording for Tom and ask him what he hears.

"It sounds like someone saying . . . something . . . 'jacket,' right?"

Since you both agree, this seems like pretty strong evidence. Now you look at the pictures. Tom looks at the picture of the chest he took right before he asked the spirit the question.

"Look at that," he says, pointing to the middle of the picture. "Do you *see* that?"

To you, it looks like an image of a man sitting on top of the chest. But on closer inspection, you're not so sure.

6. **You look closely to see if the image of the man is actually folds in the coats, or just a trick of shadows. But it's so hard to tell. Can you be sure of what you're seeing? Should you . . .**

a) **Assume that you're matrixing and move on**

b) **Take a control picture in the daylight**

c) **Shine a light from behind the picture—if it's a ghost, it will glow**

d) **Assume that it's real because the EVP occurred almost at the same time**

In each of the images with the closet in the background, the figure of the sitting man looks a little different and twisted from picture to picture. Sometimes his "face" looks sort of lumpy, and his legs don't really look the same. Because of the way it changes from picture to picture, you can tell that what you thought was a spirit was only folds in the hanging clothes. You were matrixing after all. But Tom points out that in a few pictures there are what appear to be light blue orbs.

7. **How can you tell if an orb is real, and not dust or moisture?**

a) **It has a definite border**

b) **There was nothing shiny in the background that could reflect light**

c) **The color is not entirely uniform**

d) **All of the above**

One orb image in particular has all of those qualities. Tom asks if you think maybe it was just a bug. That's possible. But it's pretty cold for bugs to be flying around. This could be a real orb. It would make sense. An orb is a ball of energy, and an energy fluctuation might have done something tricky with the lights. The time-code on the picture says it was taken right after you first started questioning the ghost. It was taken right in the middle of where the cold spot was. Putting all this together, you feel as though you have pretty strong evidence.

You've looked over all your data and you think you have a few really solid pieces of evidence. You have an EVP, a likely picture of an orb, some personal experiences, and an unexplainable cold spot. These are all strong indicators of the paranormal. Most important, you collected your evidence and reviewed it accurately. You didn't jump to conclusions, and you thought about it all rationally.

But there's one piece still missing.

8.   **What do you do with the chest of clothes?**

a)   Get rid of it, along with the spirit attached to it

b)   Use it as a tool to communicate with the spirit

c)   Forget about it and wait to see if any paranormal
     activity occurs again

d)   Experiment with it by moving it to different locations
     to see if the paranormal activity will follow it

ANSWERS

Question 1: Now that you have everything assembled, what should you do?

Answer: a) Record the time and nature of the events

This will be the official start of your investigation. It will also be important for you to have this data when analyzing the evidence to see if everything adds up.

Question 2: The light switch is not working, so you turn on the flashlight. The next thing you do is . . .

Answer: d) Turn off the TV

This is sort of a trick question. You definitely need to check to see if the lightbulb is burned out. Just because the lights went out doesn't mean your basement is haunted. What if there was a power surge in the neighborhood? But, before you do anything, you need to turn off the TV. The light from the TV would likely affect any pictures you take, and it could also affect the EMF.

Question 3: You say the date, time, and place into the recorder. What's the next thing you say?

Answer: d) Who are you?

Answer *b* is just silly, as if turning off the light in the first place was a sign. Answer *a* and answer *c* are too long. For the best results, keep it simple.

Question 4: You set the recorder right next to the vent. What happens now is up to you. What do you do?

Answer: b) Go up to the living room and experiment with the door to see if you can reproduce the noise

At this point you need to make sure that the moaning is not just coming from the creaky door. Don't forget, your first objective is to debunk a haunting.

Question 5: What will the compass tell you?

Answer: c) The compass needle will spin around, indicating that a spirit may be changing the electromagnetic field

Like an EMF detector, a compass reacts to electromagnetic fields—that's how it always points due north. Although it can't give a precise reading, if it spins around that means something strange is happening to the electromagnetic field.

Question 6: You look closely to see if the image of the man is actually folds in the coats, or just a trick of shadows. But it's so hard to tell. Can you be sure of what you're seeing? Should you . . .

Answer: b) Take a control picture in the daylight

In this case, it's easy to see if the picture is real or not. Matrixing a figure out of a cluttered coat closet is likely to happen, so you'll definitely need to compare it to a picture taken in broad daylight. While it might be tempting to assume it's real because the EVP occurred so shortly after, you cannot simply accept it as proof until you know for sure.

Question 7: How can you tell if an orb is real, and not dust or moisture?

Answer: d) All of the above

All of those qualities indicate a real orb.

Question 8: What do you do with the chest of clothes?

Answer: Any of those options are acceptable. The spirit seems not to be terribly mischievous, so it may not be necessary to get rid of the clothes. You may want to investigate further to back up the evidence you already collected.

Review: If you got the questions mostly correct, you have the right mindset to be a ghost hunter. You've got a calm, skeptical outlook, but you're also ready to find evidence of the paranormal. If you got a few questions wrong, that's okay, too. But it might be a good idea to read over the guide a few times before you investigate the famous haunted house in your neighborhood!

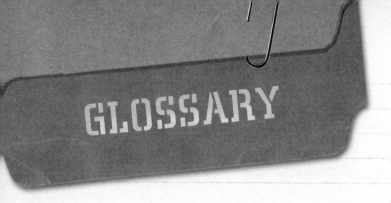

GLOSSARY

Anecdotal Evidence: Evidence of an event that comes from people's stories.

Apparition: A spirit visible to live people.

Black Mass: An apparition in the form of a shadowy black mist.

Cold Spot: A specific area where the temperature is colder than the surrounding areas, or an area where the temperature suddenly drops. Many paranormal researchers believe cold spots are caused by entities drawing energy from the air, literally sucking the heat out of the air in order to appear.

Demonic Haunting: One of the four main types of hauntings. A demonic haunting is caused by an inhuman spirit. They can be very nasty. Fortunately, they are rare.

Digital Thermometer: A device used by paranormal investigators to detect cold spots or hot spots.

Ectoplasm: A substance that's supposed to ooze out of mediums when they are in trances and are in touch with spirits. Almost no one believes it's real.

EMF Detector (Electromagnetic Field Detector): A device that records the electromagnetic field of an area (the force given off by electrical charges). Paranormal investigators use it as a tool to detect spirits either disrupting or creating electromagnetic energy. One must be careful not to measure the electromagnetic fields of common electrical sources, such as outlets, televisions, or power lines, while investigating possible paranormal activity.

Entity: A disembodied spirit.

EVP (Electronic Voice Phenomena): An audio recording of voices or sounds that, at the time of recording, were not detectable to the human ear.

Exorcism: The ceremony performed to rid an area or person of an unwelcome entity.

Geophone: A very sensitive device that "feels" vibrations on the ground and registers how strong the vibration is on a display of lights.

Ghost: See *Apparition*.

Haunting: The continued appearance of an entity at a specific location. There are four main types of hauntings: Demonic Haunting, Intelligent Haunting, Poltergeist, and Residual Haunting.

Hot Spot: An area where a lot of paranormal activity has been observed.

Infrared Camera (IR Camera): A device that uses infrared waves to see in the dark.

Inhuman Entity: A hostile entity of non-human origins.

Intelligent Haunting: One of the four main types of hauntings. An entity that has some awareness of its surroundings. It may have some limited mobility and may be able to communicate.

Ion Generator: A piece of equipment that electrically charges the air.

K-II Meter: A device that uses blinking lights to rate levels of magnetic fields and frequencies. Some paranormal investigators believe it can be used to communicate with ghosts.

Materialization: The process of an apparition becoming visible. Materialization can occur quickly or over a period of time, causing the entity to appear either solid or indistinct.

Matrixing: The tendency of the mind to add details to images that make them seem more familiar. It happens all the time, but it can cause problems when you are analyzing evidence.

Medium: A person who tries to communicate with spirits.

Negative Entity: See *Inhuman Entity*.

Orb: A floating sphere, often white or bluish, that shows up in a photograph or video. An orb is a contained ball of energy. Some consider an orb to be evidence of paranormal activity. It is often confused with dust, bugs, or an optical illusion registering on film or video.

Ouija Board: A board with letters, numbers, and symbols printed on a smooth surface. It is used to try to communicate with spirits.

Paranormal: Literally "beyond normal." Something paranormal is an event or phenomenon that is beyond what is normally experienced by humans—or what can be scientifically explained.

Paranormal Indicator: Evidence that may lead one to believe paranormal activity has taken place.

Paranormal Investigator: Also called a ghost hunter. A person who gathers information and evidence about paranormal activity.

Phantom Smell: An odor caused by a spirit attempting to make itself known. Common phantom smells include flowers, tobacco, or perfume. A phantom smell is considered paranormal only if it cannot be traced to a source.

Poltergeist: One of the four main types of hauntings. A ghost that moves objects to draw attention to itself. Banging sounds often accompany the movements. The phenomenon often revolves around an individual person, usually a child.

Possession: An instance where an inhuman entity enters a human and influences that person's behavior and personality for a period of time.

Residual Haunting: One of the four main types of hauntings. An entity will replay a moment from the recent or distant past at the exact location where it happened. Usually the entity does not have any recognition of the living people watching it.

Sensitive: Any person with a sensitivity to the paranormal.

Thermal Camera: An IR camera that makes cold and heat visible.

Vortex: A gateway from the spirit world into the physical world.

VP (Voice Phenomena): Sounds or voices heard during an investigation that have no natural cause.

Warm Spot: Similar to a cold spot, a warm spot is an area that is hotter than its surrounding areas. Some investigators believe spirits using energy to show themselves create warmth, almost like a body does.

ACKNOWLEDGMENTS

We want to thank Jody Hotchkiss at Hotchkiss and Associates for making all these things possible. Without your guidance, none of this could have happened.

Special thanks to Jane Stine from Parachute Publishing; your faith in us has allowed us the chances we have today.

Thanks to Craig Paligian and Alan David from Pilgrim Films and Television for taking a chance on us in 2004 that allowed us to change the way the paranormal would be looked at from then on.

And to Rob Katz, who has proven to be a true friend and the best executive producer in the field.

And thanks, too, to David Axelrod for his work on the *Ghost Hunt* Guide and his other valuable contributions to this book.

And to Little, Brown, you have given us a chance to prove our love for what we do; for this we are always in your debt.

JASON HAWES and **GRANT WILSON** have been avid investigators of the paranormal for more than twenty years and have investigated over two thousand claims of paranormal activity, helping families, law enforcement agencies, the military, and churches do both preliminary and extensive investigations. They are the bestselling authors of the books *Ghost Hunting* and *Seeking Spirits* for adults, and they are best known for their television show, *Ghost Hunters*, on Syfy and for being the founder and the cofounder, respectively, of The Atlantic Paranormal Society (TAPS). Jason Hawes was born in Canandaigua, New York, and now lives in Rhode Island with his wife and five children. Grant Wilson was born and raised in Providence, Rhode Island, where he continues to live with his wife and three boys.

Get **MORE Chills, MORE Thrills, MORE Ghosts!**

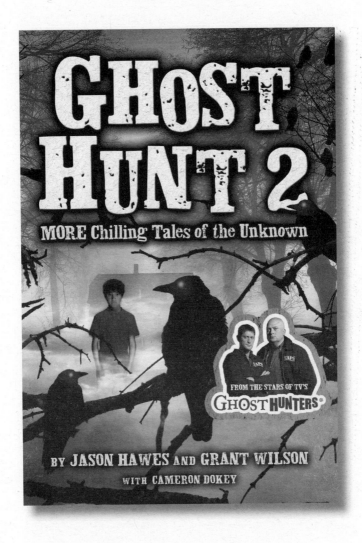

Turn the page for a sneak peek!

LOST IN THE LAKE

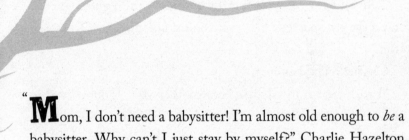

"Mom, I don't need a babysitter! I'm almost old enough to *be* a babysitter. Why can't I just stay by myself?" Charlie Hazelton glared at her mother. "I'm twelve," she said. "I mean, come *on*."

"Charlie, this is a new place. I don't think it's a good idea for you to be alone," Charlie's mother said.

From the way she said it, Charlie could tell that her mother hadn't made up her mind. Charlie still had a chance if she could talk fast enough.

"All you're going to do is run some errands, right? It's not like you'll be gone all that long."

"Most of the afternoon," Mrs. Hazelton said. "Which is long enough. I have to buy all the food for the housewarming party on Sunday. And it takes a while to get into town." Mrs. Hazelton sighed. "Sometimes I wonder what your father and I were thinking, moving way out into the country like this."

All of a sudden, her expression brightened. "Hey, maybe you should come along. You know, a shopping trip. Just you and me. Wouldn't that be fun?"

"Mom," Charlie said. "You're going to the *grocery store,* not the mall."

"Oh, all right." Her mother abruptly gave in. "I guess you can stay here by yourself. On one condition: stay away from the lake."

Charlie rolled her eyes.

"I really mean it, Charlie," her mother said. "You've lived in apartments your whole life. You didn't even learn to swim until last year. And we don't know how deep the lake is. I'm just not comfortable with you going down there on your own."

"I got my junior lifesaving certificate," Charlie reminded her. "Mom, I'm *twelve.* You know—almost a teenager." How many times did she have to say it before her mother got the point?

"There are stories about that lake," Mrs. Hazelton went on. Clearly, she wasn't really listening to Charlie at all.

"What kind of stories?" Charlie asked.

"I don't know," her mother said impatiently. "I've just heard that no one swims there. It's not safe. Now, either you promise not to go near the lake or you come with me."

"Oh, all right," Charlie said. "Honestly."

If I ever have kids, I won't treat them like babies, she thought. *It's embarrassing sometimes.*

Forget that. It's embarrassing all *the time.*

"Promise me," her mother said.

"Mom."

"*Promise* me," her mother insisted.

Charlie sighed. "I promise not to go near the lake," she said. "There! Okay?"

She meant to keep her promise. She honestly did. But her mom never said she had to stay inside. Right?

Right, Charlie thought. She stepped onto the front porch and closed the door behind her. She had lived here for exactly one week. Her parents dragged her away from her friends, her school…everything! So Charlie figured that she had a right to go exploring.

She walked down the porch steps and turned left. Her sneakers made soft swooshing sounds as she crossed the lawn. It was smooth and green, like a carpet. Charlie thought it was fake the first time she saw it.

She went around the corner of the house and headed for the orchard. It was pretty—if you liked rows and rows of apple trees. After the orchard came the meadow. It was on a hill, sloping down. At the bottom of the meadow was the lake.

The one that she was supposed to stay away from.

"I don't know what Mom's so worried about," Charlie muttered to herself. She stomped through the orchard. "It's not even a real lake. More like a pond. It's probably not even deep."

Still, to play it safe, Charlie stopped at the top of the hill. She could see the lake from there. Which was definitely *not* the same as breaking her promise. Mom never said that Charlie couldn't *look* at the lake.

The water looked quiet and peaceful in the summer sunshine.

Okay. It probably is big enough to be called a lake, Charlie thought. It even looked deep. But it didn't look dangerous.

The lake curved around in a funny shape, like an enormous kidney bean. The water was green and clear. The biggest willow tree Charlie had ever seen stood on the far shore. The tree's long, skinny branches draped down like a pale green curtain. Some of the tree's roots were actually underwater.

Charlie couldn't see the roots from where she stood. But her dad had told her about them.

A breeze came up. It ruffled the surface of the water, making it sparkle in the sun. Then there was a quick, blinding flash of light. Charlie cried out in surprise and covered her eyes.

When she uncovered them, she saw the little boy.

He looked as if he was about five years old. He wore a red

T-shirt and baggy jeans. He was standing about halfway down the hill, staring at the lake.

Who is he? What's he doing out here all by himself? Charlie wondered. *Does he live around here?*

No, she answered her own question. No one lived around here. The nearest neighbors lived over a mile away. And they didn't have kids.

"Hey!" she called.

The boy turned his head to look at her.

"What's your name?" Charlie yelled. "What are you doing around here?"

The boy didn't answer. Instead, he began to run.

He ran down the slope, toward the water.

"Wait up!" Charlie called. "I didn't mean to sound mad. I just..."

For such a little kid, he was running really fast. He ran down a steep, skinny path. He nearly tripped. But he kept running.

"Hey, watch out!" Charlie called. "Watch where you're going—or at least slow down!"

But the boy didn't slow down. He ran even faster, straight toward the lake. It was almost as if something was chasing him—or as if he couldn't stop.

Charlie didn't know why exactly, but something felt bad. The boy was so little. What if he couldn't swim? What if the lake was seriously deep? What if it really *was* dangerous?

What if he *was* being chased — by something she couldn't see?

Charlie forgot her promise to her mother and sprinted after the boy. She ran as fast as she could, but the hill was super-steep. It was hard to go fast without falling. She didn't understand how the boy could be running so quickly.

She forced herself to run faster. She felt a sharp pain in her left side. Her heart pounded hard. The boy was still running, almost to the edge of the water.

"Stop!" Charlie shouted. "I just want to talk to you. Please, stop!"

But even as she ran faster than she ever did before, she knew it wasn't going to do any good. The boy was too far ahead, and Charlie was never going to get to him in time.

And then the miracle happened. The boy stopped right at the edge of the lake. But Charlie couldn't. She was going too fast. She tried to stop, but the lakeshore was muddy. It grabbed on to her sneakers and held them tight.

Her momentum was too great and she plunged face-first into the water. Instantly, her shorts and shirt and running shoes were soaking wet and cold.

The water shot straight up Charlie's nose. It smelled like dead fish. She grasped at the bottom of the lake, trying to push herself up. But the bottom of the lake was soft and muddy, and her hands sank into thick, squishy mud.

Swim, she told herself. She knew how to swim. She tried to straighten and kick. But all she did was churn up mud. The water was a dark, murky brown. She couldn't tell where the top or bottom was. Slimy weeds wrapped around her leg. They were pulling her down, holding her under. Charlie's chest felt tight. She was almost out of breath!

Then, all of a sudden, her hands hit something hard. A big rock. Charlie pushed. Her head came out of the water. Charlie gulped air.

It's all right, she thought. *I'm all right.*

But she was going to be in so much trouble.

Her mom was never going to understand. She would think Charlie deliberately broke her promise.

But I didn't! Charlie thought. *I was just trying to help that little boy.*

The boy. Where was he?

With a great *whoosh* of water, Charlie staggered to her feet. She spun around. The boy was standing on the bank behind her.

"What are you doing here all by yourself?" Charlie asked. "Why did you run that way? Were you *trying* to scare me half to death? Are you all right?"

The boy didn't say anything. He just stood there, staring at Charlie with big, brown eyes. His skin was super-pale. As though he never went out in the sun.

"Who are you, anyway?" Charlie said. *"What do you want?"*

At that moment, a gust of wind came up. Charlie felt it lift the hair away from her face. It pushed her wet clothes tight against her body. She began to shiver uncontrollably. But not because she was cold.

The boy's hair. The boy's clothes. They didn't move at all.

But he did. He raised one arm. His hand was clenched into a fist. Then, slowly, one finger uncurled. His index finger. It pointed, straight at the lake. Then his whole body gave this funny sort of ripple. As if he were made out of smoke. But his finger never moved. It kept pointing at the lake.

Then, just like that, the boy was gone.

Charlie sat back down in the water.

She didn't care that her clothes were soaked. She didn't care about the trouble she was going to be in when she got home.

All she cared about was the image in her head. The little boy pointing at the water. And along with seeing the image, she heard a voice that seemed to be carried by the cold wind.

It circled around and around in Charlie's brain. Like it was looking for a way back out but couldn't find one.

Find me, the voice in Charlie's head said over and over and over. *Find me. I'm here.*

Find me.

Find me.

FIND ME.

It was the voice of a little boy.

"Let me be clear, right up front," Mr. Hazelton said. "I don't believe in ghosts."

"That's okay," Grant answered. His tone was friendly. "A lot of people —"

"Because I don't want you to think that's why we called you," Mr. Hazelton went on. "I don't want *you* to think it's because *we* think we actually have a ghost. We just want to check things out."

Lyssa bit down on her tongue to keep from smiling.

"Of course you do." Grant finally managed to get a word in edgewise. "As I explained when you phoned, we are here just to investigate. We don't come in with our minds already made up about what we might find. We never try to prove that there is a haunting. In fact, we try to prove there isn't."

"Good," Mr. Hazelton said. "Well, that's all right, then. We understand each other."

There was a pause. Now that he'd made his point, Mr. Hazelton didn't seem to know what else to say. He glanced over at his wife. She was sitting beside him on the couch. Their daughter, Charlie, sat next to her mother.

Jay, Grant, and Lyssa were sitting in chairs across from the Hazeltons in the family's living room. The rest of the TAPS team were outside unloading the equipment. There was a lot of gear. The team would be investigating both inside the house and out by the lake.

Charlie doesn't look particularly happy to be here, Lyssa thought. In fact, she looked like she would rather be someplace else.

"I'd like to ask Charlie a question, if that's okay," Lyssa said.

The girl lifted her eyes. They were a blue so dark they looked almost black. The expression in them seemed to ask Lyssa a question first: *Can I trust you?*

"Go ahead," Mr. Hazelton said.

"Charlie, you're the only one who has seen the little boy," Lyssa said. "Is that right?"

"Yeah," Charlie said. "I've seen him lots of times. I keep trying to tell *them.*" Charlie jerked her chin toward her parents. "They don't believe me."

"We're trying to believe you, honey," her mother said. "We know leaving all your friends back in Chicago was hard. It's not unusual to imagine things when everything is new and strange..." Mrs. Hazelton's voice trailed off.

"I saw him. He's real," Charlie insisted.

"The first time Charlie told us about the boy was after she did something she wasn't supposed to do," Mr. Hazelton put in. "So naturally we wondered if she was making it up. You know, telling a story to get out of trouble."

"I *explained* what happened—" Charlie began.

"I have a question for you, Charlie," Jason cut in quickly. The girl's eyes shot to his face. As always, Jason's expression was steady and calm.

"What?"

"Is the lake the only place you've seen the boy?"

Charlie nodded. "Uh-huh. I don't go near the water anymore. But I can see him from the hill. He isn't always there, though. Just sometimes. I think Roscoe sees him, too."

"Who's Roscoe?" Lyssa asked.

"Our dog. He comes with me when I go for walks. But sometimes he goes down to the lake on his own. Then all he does is just sit there and howl."

"Does he howl anywhere else?" Jen asked.

Charlie nodded. "Yeah, sometimes. Right outside my room. He always does it when the door to my room locks itself and I get stuck inside. That's pretty freaky, I have to tell you."

"Charlie," Mr. Hazelton said. His voice sounded worried and frustrated all at the same time. "Honey, we've been over this. Your door can't lock itself. It doesn't even *have* a lock."

Charlie shot to her feet. "Fine. Make me sound stupid. You're always right. I'm always wrong. But guess what?"

"Charlie," her mother murmured. But Charlie kept right on going.

"I think you know there's something weird going on around here," she said to her father. "You just don't want to admit it.

Because then *you'd* be wrong. Wrong about making us move here in the first place!"

Charlie swung around. Her eyes locked on Lyssa's. "That little boy is out there," she said. "I *saw* him. He needs us to find him. If you won't help him, I'll do it myself."

She dashed from the room. A moment later, the front door slammed.

"Charlie!" Mrs. Hazelton called, alarmed.

"I'll go after her," Lyssa said. She got to her feet. "Don't worry. I'll find her."

"Lyssa is our chief interviewer," Grant explained to Mr. and Mrs. Hazelton. "Sometimes kids tell her more when she talks to them on her own. So while she talks to Charlie, maybe you can give us some more details about what's been going on up at the house."

"All right. We can do that, can't we, Ray?" Mrs. Hazelton said.

"We can do whatever it takes," Mr. Hazelton said. His voice was grim. "But you just remember what I said."

"I remember," Grant said. "You don't believe in ghosts..."